The Proud and The Beast:
A Pride and Prejudice Variation

By

Kate Speck

For Scott

Chapter 1

"What in damnation?!" Darcy yelled, as he saw the gigantic tree at Oakham Mount suddenly move and twist its long limbs to attack him.

He pulled the reins hard, causing his horse to rear up, and as Darcy leaned back to dodge the swinging branch, his horse neighed loudly and shook its head from the unexpected actions of its master. In the confusion and chaos, Darcy lost his seat and was thrown off his stallion, landing on his side and bumping his head on the solid ground. All Darcy could think of was his dear sister as his world darkened.

Darcy began to regain consciousness as he felt a soft hand on his head.

"Sir, sir, can you open your eyes? Can you hear me?" He heard the voice call out.

He groaned, as he felt sharp pain in his head. He could not understand what happened and it hurt to try to open his eyes.

The voice grew louder. "Sir, you were thrown off your horse. Can you move? Open your eyes." The feminine voice called again.

Darcy felt a hand pressing onto his temple and slowly opened his eyes to find a hideous creature over him and he screamed in horror. "Do not touch me! Who are you? What are you doing to me?" He raised his arms and attempted to sit up to distance himself from her but could not rise due to his pains.

The voice was gentle but this monster looked like an evil witch with freckles and a deformed face. Her face was scarred as if burned and he cringed in disgust.

"Be calm, be calm! Do not worry, sir. I am not here to hurt you. I am not doing anything to you but trying to help. I will not compromise you, if you are so concerned," the voice sharply replied, "I am only trying to stop the bleeding. You must stop moving!" She gently chastised him.

Darcy closed his eyes again. Everything looked strange and although the creature was fearsome in her appearance, her voice was soothing and it calmed him.

"Thank you for your help. Blasted! I do not remember what happened. I honestly do not have a recollection of being on my horse. Do you see him near?" Darcy asked quietly, attempting to ascertain how such a monstrosity could exist and be out of doors, or if his mind was playing a trick on him.

"Yes, your stallion is about fifty yards away. I was taking my morning walk and saw your horse rear for no reason at all. It almost appeared as if you were frightened by something or being attacked, and I witnessed you fall off. You are bleeding from your head. Can you move your limbs?" She saw him wiggle his arms and legs to test them out. "What is your name, sir? Where are you staying? Are you by chance part of the Netherfield party?" The voice asked smoothly while her hand was still pressing the side of his head.

"I am Fitzwilliam Darcy. I am visiting my friend Bingley. Yes, Netherfield is the name. I do not remember when I arrived here and I cannot recollect much right now. My head hurts so much and I feel ill." Darcy was nauseous and dizzy.

"You bumped your head quite hard, I believe. Your bleeding is slowing. Do you think you can sit up?" She inquired.

Darcy slowly opened his eyes again. The world was still spinning but not as much as before. That horrendous being was hovering over him and although repulsive, he noted the sparkle in her eyes and concentrated on that.

"You are very loathsome in appearance but kind. I thank you for your assistance. What are you called?" Darcy bluntly asked.

The creature laughed loudly. "You insult me and thank me. I will attribute your terrible manners to your injury and will not take too much offense. Since we have already foregone propriety, you may call me 'Lizzy'. Can you sit up?"

"I will try. Help me up, Lizzy." He felt her hand behind his neck. Darcy slowly arose, with one hand on Lizzy's shoulder and the other on the ground to lift himself up. He looked around and the colors began to brighten into normal shades and not so frightening like before, but he could still see the trees swaying.

"What is that?!" Darcy yelled, as he pointed to another monster at a distance. Instinctively, he held on to Lizzy, unsure if to protect her or to hide himself behind her.

"That is your horse, Mr. Darcy. Why should you be afraid of your own horse?" Lizzy inquired curiously.

"I see a monster. Nothing appears as it seems, Lizzy." Darcy shakily responded and looked around his surroundings. "It looks like a monster to me, as do the trees."

"I think this is more than your head being injured, Mr. Darcy. You will need to rest and be seen by a doctor." Lizzy furrowed her brows in concern. "I have never heard of envisioning monsters after a head wound."

"Have you seen many head wounds, Lizzy?" Darcy asked, still holding on to this kind beast. "I could swear that you appear a monster to me right now and if I had a sword, I might have run you through in fear." Darcy commented, blinking several times to see if his vision would alter. He lifted his hand to touch her face with one finger to ascertain if she was real.

"I only have read of head injuries and I do not have practical knowledge I may not be beautiful but I have not been accused of appearing so hideous that I should be locked in the dungeons." Lizzy laughed, as her nose and cheeks were being poked by the gentleman's finger.

Darcy squeezed Lizzy's shoulders and arms, and felt flesh and bones. She was petite but firm and strong. "You feel like a human, even if you do not appear as one. Why are you being so kind to me?" He looked into her eyes as he continued to sit only inches away from her.

"It is what people do, do they not? Any decent being would have stopped to help you." Lizzy responded.

Darcy scoffed, "No, Lizzy, not everyone. Many would have robbed me and left me for dead. Some *ladies* might not get near me in fear of dirtying their dresses or faint at the sight of blood. You are very brave and compassionate to help a stranger."

"I do not know where you are from, but I should hope that those in my neighborhood would help a stranger in need. I do know many ladies who faint at the sight of blood, like my mother for instance, but my courage rises at every challenge. I have taken care of many bumps and scrapes, fortunately for you, and I do not mind getting a little dirty." She smiled.

Darcy saw her smile and although Lizzy's face still appeared deformed, it began to take a different shape, resembling more that of a lady than a monster.

"You are still hideous but have a pretty smile, Lizzy." Darcy honestly commented.

Lizzy blushed at the compliment. "Thank you. You have a very nice smile as well, Mr. Darcy."

Darcy did not realize he was smiling at her and was startled to the present. He recalled that his head was wounded, she was a horribly disfigured oddity, and he was clearly hallucinating everything. *This must be a dream. A horrible nightmare! I must get back to Bingley's estate.*

"Well, if you will bring my horse closer, I believe I can ride back to Netherfield. My head is not spinning as much now, although everything still looks frightful." Darcy stated, as he still held on to Lizzy's shoulder and shook his head to test out his equilibrium.

"Do I still look loathsome to you?" Lizzy asked, comprehending that this handsome gentleman might be suffering from delusions and not meaning to insult her appearances so severely.

"Yes, Lizzy, your face is still frightful but you have beautiful eyes. Very fine, indeed." He cradled her cheek and held it in his palm. He was surprised at the attachment he felt for this gentle soul, and he leaned closer, wishing to taste her scarred lips. He released her quickly and cleared his throat, snapping to his current situation. "If you will get my horse to me, I must return."

Lizzy smiled at his discomfort. He had been holding her more intimately than appropriate but he did not seem like a rake. "Yes, I will get your horse. You are fortunate he did not run off far. You must keep pressing here," she lifted his hand to his temple where she had been pressing with her handkerchief, "and I will return shortly."

Lizzy stood and approached the stallion carefully and after petting its head, she grabbed the reins and walked back to where Darcy was sitting.

"Help me stand, Lizzy." Darcy commanded, as he placed the bloodied handkerchief into his pocket.

Lizzy rolled her eyes in amusement, "As you wish, sir."

Darcy slowly placed his feet on the ground and raised himself, wrapping one arm around Lizzy's shoulders. After standing and finding himself quite dizzy, he closed his eyes again and took several deep breaths while holding on to the kind creature.

Lizzy was quite uncomfortable with being so enwrapped in this gentleman's arms. Not only was his arm embracing her shoulders, his other arm had found itself around her back and he left no room between his body and hers. His head was touching hers and she could feel his warm breath on her ear. Her arms were around him to help him stabilize and she realized that he was swaying a little, still unbalanced.

"Come, sir. Let us get you on your horse." Lizzy requested. "You might go around embracing women where you come from, but this is quite uncomfortable for me, Mr. Darcy." She jokingly commented.

His eyes opening slowly, he tersely replied, "I would never take advantage of a servant. You are safe with me, Lizzy." He released her abruptly, pulled out a guinea from his waistcoat and placed it on her palm. "For your service today. Thank you. If you come to Netherfield later, I will reward you with a ten-pound note for your troubles."

Lizzy scoffed at the presumption. She had never been so thoroughly insulted in one day. "I do not need your money, sir. As a daughter of a *gentleman*, I have no need for employment." She attempted to return the coin back to Darcy.

Darcy colored at his faux pas, and reaching for her freckled and deformed hand, he used both of his hands to close it into a fist. He looked into her eyes again and found her appearance even more tolerable now. "I apologize, Lizzy. I meant no insult. Please keep it. I am truly grateful for your assistance." He lifted her hand and kissed it. He turned around and saw his monstrous horse and cringed. Something was definitely not right with his mind.

"You are welcome, Mr. Darcy. I wish you safe travel back to Netherfield. If you follow that way," she pointed towards the mansion's direction, "it will get you back in two miles."

He nodded and reached for the saddle. With the expertise of a life-long rider, he easily hopped onto the saddle and grabbed the reins.

"Get me back home, Perseus." Darcy patted his trusty stallion. The horse nodded his head as if to answer and began its trot. Darcy looked back and called out to Lizzy, "Thank you, Miss Lizzy."

Lizzy waved her hand in farewell and began her journey home. This had been an interesting day. Very interesting, indeed.

Chapter 2

Darcy heard a faint noise next to him that began to grow louder as he became more aware of his surroundings. The voice grew louder and he recognized it as his sister reading from a book. His head was piercing with sharp pain and he could not recall why his head would hurt so much.

"Geo..." Darcy croaked, his mouth too dry to make more noise.

Georgiana jumped up from her reading. "William! I am so glad you are awake!" She began to cry. "I thought I was going to lose you, dear brother." She hugged him and helped him with a sip of water after sitting him up slightly.

Darcy smiled softly. "You will not lose me, sweetling. What has happened? Where am I?" He looked around and did not recognize the bedroom.

Georgiana gasped in shock. "You are in Hertfordshire, at Mr. Bingley's home, Netherfield. Do you not remember?"

"Hertfordshire? When did I get here? I was supposed to go to Bingley's new home after Michaelmas." Darcy asked in bewilderment.

"William, you arrived here five days ago. Today is the fourth of October. You travelled here on Monday and you had an accident on Tuesday morning. I was told that you went for a ride and came back with blood on your head then you lost consciousness and have been sleeping for three days. I must call for our doctor. Give me one minute, Brother." Georgiana informed him, then arose to talk to the footman outside the door.

After returning, she sat next to her brother's bed and held his hand. "Mr. Bingley was extremely concerned and sent me an express and I have been here since Tuesday evening. You have been very ill but I am so happy to see you awake." She began to cry again.

Darcy lay in confusion as he tried to recall the past week. He remembered clearly being at Darcy House and then nothing. He had a flash of memory of seeing a colossal tree swinging its branches and then looking into the most beautiful pair of eyes, but nothing else surfaced.

"Did you arrive here alone? Where is Mrs. Annesley?" Darcy asked in concern, his thoughts returning to the present and becoming anxious over his sister's safety and comfort above all else.

Georgiana smiled at her brother's care. "I am here with Mrs. Annesley and Richard, William. Richard took leave as soon as he heard the news and accompanied us here. Mrs. Annesley is resting and Richard has been sitting with you for hours but Mr. Bingley finally convinced him to play a game of billiards to take a break."

Darcy sighed in relief. "I am glad you did not arrive alone. We do not know where... *he* is located, and I do not wish for you to be alone. My head aches but I am feeling better," he reached for his sister's hand, "now that you are with me. I am glad Richard is here as well."

Then, there was a knock at the door and Georgiana answered it.

"Hey! Look who is finally awake!" Richard jovially remarked. "The doctor said you should awaken any time but of course you took your lazy time to take a very long nap."

In truth, Colonel Richard Fitzwilliam had been seriously worried for his cousin. Being an army officer, he had seen a number of men severely wounded in the head, and some would either remain comatose until death overtook them, or their mind would become befuddled and debilitated, unable to function more than like a child.

Bingley laughed and commented, "Of course Darcy is not lazy! I have never seen him indolent in all the years I have known him!"

"Darcy, can you tell us what happened? Do you know where you are?" Richard asked carefully, seeing a slight haze in his cousin's eyes.

Darcy snorted, "I believe I earned a little sleep, Richard. I recall you being in bed for a fortnight when you returned from the continent."

Richard smiled in relief, hearing Darcy speak clearly and quite lucid, "Well, I was shot in the leg and could not walk so I had a perfect excuse! How are you feeling?"

"I am told I am at Netherfield but I do not remember arriving. Georgiana has been telling me that I had an accident on Tuesday after going riding but I do not recollect arriving in Hertfordshire in the first place. I only recall still being at Darcy House and it being still September." Darcy spoke slowly and drank a sip of wine that Georgiana offered.

Bingley spoke next to fill him in. "I saw you before your ride that morning, Darcy. You appeared quite upset about something but you did not say anything to me and then you left. Caroline was with us and served you a hot cup of coffee and you took off soon after. When you returned, you were barely holding on to your horse and had blood on your head. Your wound was oozing and you were unable to open your eyes. I had several men carry you in and you vomited twice then lost consciousness. I called for the surgeon who came to examine you within the hour and I sent off an express to Miss Darcy that same morning. The surgeon told me that your head wound needed stitches and looked over the rest of your body to find it sound."

Richard continued the story, "After Georgie and I arrived, it appeared that we could not awaken you, even with smelling salts, so we sent for your personal doctor to examine you. Hastings arrived the next day and found bruising on your hip and shoulder and he surmised that you fell off your horse and landed on the ground quite hard. He has gone into the local town here to see if anyone might have witnessed your injury perchance, and should return shortly."

Darcy closed his eyes and recalled a feminine voice speaking to him but he could not discern who she was or what had been said.

"Darcy! Are you well?" Bingley asked loudly.

"I will be fine as long as you do not shout, Charles." Darcy gruffly replied. "Could you please send in my valet? I would like to wash and change my clothes." He opened his eyes and turned to his family and friend. "Thank you for your care. Bingley, thank you for calling for my family. I am comforted to have them near me."

Bingley smiled broadly, "It is the least I could do, Darcy. I am glad to see you awaken. I will have the doctor examine you as soon as he returns."

Georgiana kissed her brother's cheek, "I will ask for a tray to be delivered. You must be famished. Some soup to start with, William. I will return soon."

Richard squeezed his cousin's hand, "See you in a bit. Rest, cousin."

The visitors quickly excused themselves for Darcy's ablutions and to call for nourishments to be delivered as quickly as possible.

As Wilkins, his valet, was helping him, Darcy thought of the blank memory of the past few days and most importantly, what might had happened after he arrived, up until his injury. There were about thirty-six hours of his life that he could not account for and it was maddening!

Chapter 3

"Thank you for staying with me. I know you would rather be with Miss Bingley at the assembly and all of her compliments to you, but I am glad to have your company." Darcy teased his sister.

Georgiana laughed, "William, you must not taunt me! You know Miss Bingley has been driving me absolutely insane for over a week! How one could have so much to praise for something so miniscule is incredible to me. She extols my accomplishments over my table decoration and my dress, to the choice of my ribbons and my being born a Darcy, as if I have achieved world peace. The word 'accomplished' is applied to many of women who do not deserve it."

Darcy joined her in laughter. "I believe her list of the common extent of accomplishments only applies to those of noble birth and wealth. By that definition alone, you are more accomplished than anyone else with whom she is acquainted! What is your idea of an accomplished woman, Georgiana?"

"I understand a woman must have a thorough knowledge of music, singing, drawing, dancing, and the modern languages, but a truly accomplished woman must also be wise and kind. I know that I have much to learn and I am most thankful that you allow me to read histories and philosophies to improve my mind. Outer beauty will fade in time, but true inner beauty, that of generosity and intelligence, will last a lifetime, whether for my own benefit or for my future family's." Georgiana confidently stated.

Darcy's mind drifted with her words as another memory flashed in his mind.

'You are very loathsome in appearance but kind.' He recalled uttering those words to a woman with a deformed, freckled face. He saw a beautiful set of eyes and felt a feeling of calmness in her care.

Who is she? She was the most grotesque woman I had seen and yet her inner beauty was more beautiful than anyone I had ever met.

"Are you well, William?" Georgiana broke his reverie.

Darcy turned and saw his sister. He smiled, "My mind wandered for a moment with a memory; I am not sure if it was a dream or reality, but I am well. You are beautiful, sweetling. No matter how one looks on the outside, kindness and a good heart is what matters most, is it not? You have inner beauty as well as outer beauty, and someday, some long, long days away from now, you will make a deserving man very happy." He squeezed her hand. "Now, tell me more about Uncle and Aunt Matlock. Have they been driving Richard insane?"

Georgiana smiled and informed him of their relatives and how they were pressing their cousin to marry soon. They spent the next hour conversing pleasantly until Darcy needed to rest once again.

~~*~*~*~*

"Congratulate me! I believe I have found my future wife, Darcy!" Colonel Fitzwilliam excitedly chimed, as he walked into Darcy's room, seeing that he was awake and partaking nourishment with Georgiana.

Darcy rolled his eyes. "Congratulations. This is what, your fifth future wife?"

Georgiana laughed. "Congratulations, Richard. I hope you are successful with *this* lady."

"Well, I think I am in love but alas, she is no heiress and I will need to find a way to make a fortune if I do not wish to give up my comforts. Bingley and I can become brothers when he marries her sister." Richard smiled.

"Oh, of course, and Bingley fell in love as well. That would be his...

fifteenth… future wife?" Darcy laughed. "He falls in and out of love more often than you!"

Richard laughed heartily. "True, so true, but since he has no impediments to wealth, he will be successful. Bingley's lady is very beautiful but she appears too calm for my taste. MY lady, on the other hand, is quite pretty and witty. She and I conversed for a long while and I believe she will be a great friend to Georgiana. Our ward here, Darcy, has been suffering too long at your bedside and deserves some company of worthy ladies nearer her age. And NOT Miss Bingley." Richard laughed. "I like Bingley well-enough, but that shrew is as stuck-up as I have ever seen. She implied to a few of her neighbors at the assembly that her *almost betrothed* was ill at Netherfield and that was why she was not dancing with anyone, and I had to put her in her place, telling them that my *cousin,* who remains quite single and unattached, was recovering from an illness and chose to remain here, and she shut her mouth very quickly then."

Darcy frowned, "What is she thinking? If she is besmirching my reputation before I have even met any of these residents, I will need to have Bingley speak with her. I will not tolerate such rumors. As soon as I am recovered, perhaps we will return to Pemberley," he looked at Georgiana. "We would be happier at home."

"I know, William. I do wish to be at home. I believe I can tolerate returning there where… where I will not think of *him* so much now." Georgiana sullenly replied.

She had been quite miserable at Pemberley this past summer when she had returned home after the Ramsgate event. She could not decide if her misery was due to her heartbreak of George Wickham's desiring to marry her for her 30,000-pound dowry, or if it was because she had to be hostess to Miss Bingley and Mrs. Hurst for a full month. She had been relieved to return to London to stay with Lord and Lady Matlock to concentrate on her music studies the past few months and had kept herself quite busy.

Richard hugged his ward affectionately, "It will all be well, Georgie. Perhaps my *future wife* will become a good friend to you and she can visit Pemberley with you." He joked.

Georgiana quickly wiped her tears and smiled. "You are both the best guardians I could wish for. I am so grateful for you both. I will retire now. Good night, William. Good night, Richard."

After Georgiana departed, Richard sat closer and asked, "So, how have you been, Darcy? Any memories returning?"

"I had a few visions appear but I do not know if it was a dream. I keep seeing a hideous creature with beautiful brown eyes looking over me and I remember telling her that she was loathsome but kind. I felt a connection to that… that monster… for some reason but I cannot recall anything else." Darcy stared into the canopy over his bed. He could see those eyes again and his heart thumped a little harder.

"Her? You fell for a monstrous beast with pretty eyes? Will wonders never cease?" Richard laughed. "It sounds as if your future wife will be ugly and my future wife will be poor." Richard's thoughts returned to the beauty he met tonight. "Miss Bennet is very lively and made me smile. She was easy to speak with and although her mother was quite uncouth, I could see myself marrying a woman like that. If only she had a decent dowry… What do you think, Darcy? Would my parents be pleased with my marrying a penniless daughter of an obscure gentleman with 2,000 a year?" He laughed at Darcy's frown.

Darcy haughtily replied, "Absolutely not! You need someone with a large dowry. At least 10,000 pounds, to live comfortably as a son of an earl. Georgiana has been telling me that they wish you to marry soon but no matter what pretty face, you need a wife who will bring something to be a daughter of an earl."

"I know, I know. Even with all their pressures of marriage, I do not think they would approve of this lady." He sighed. "But, hey…" Richard thought for a moment, "she is someone well-suited for a grouchy fellow... like *you*… wait a minute… I think… I think I have the perfect future wife for YOU!"

Darcy laughed loudly at Richard's sudden change of disposition. "First, she was *your* future wife, then you laugh at *my* future wife's ugliness, and now this lady of yours will be MY future wife? You have had too much to drink, cousin. Perhaps I will take Bingley's future wife instead. Haha! Richard, you know I need a wife who will be a good mistress for Pemberley as well as one who will care for Georgiana. I could never marry one unfit for the position. Even if beautiful, there are several criteria to be Mrs. Darcy of Pemberley and a lady with no dowry and no connections would never do."

Darcy's thoughts drifted to the kind eyes. *I could never take a wife who could not be presented in public. Whether kind or intelligent, her inner beauty is not enough.* He despaired at the hypocrisy that he had just shared with his sister.

Richard interrupted his thoughts. "Since when did you have a need to fill your coffers, Darcy? You sound as pompous as my parents. Well, I plan on calling on her tomorrow with Bingley. I will spy on her for you and report back to you on her suitability. I truly believe she will be a good friend to Georgie and I definitely think she would make you a good wife." Richard patted his cousin's shoulder. "Rest, cousin. I am glad you are recovering well. Wilkins will sit with you again tonight in case you need anything. We have had to bar Caroline Bingley from entering your rooms several times and although she would not dare try to compromise you with Georgie and me here, I am not taking any chances. She has been behaving more oddly than her wont." He chuckled. "That is one woman that we would both never consider as a future wife, no matter her beauty or fortune. I would rather marry that beast of yours. Good night."

After the colonel left, Darcy thought of another flash of memory, this time containing Caroline Bingley in a nightgown.

What in blazes?! Did I really see her in a nightgown? He shuddered. *Truly, she is one I would never consider appropriate. She is handsome enough but she looks too much like Bingley! She cares for no one but herself and is as mercenary as they come.*

His thoughts flew back to the creature. *Who is she? Why can I not stop thinking of her and her gorgeous eyes? Even with her disfigurement, I found her attractive. Something is seriously wrong with me.*

Darcy was determined to get out of his room tomorrow and investigate for himself what might have happened to him. Being a skillful rider since a young boy, there was no way he fell off his horse simply by accident.

Chapter 4

"Mr. Darcy!" Caroline Bingley cooed. She carefully approached him and quickly sat on the chair across from him in the library. "How are you feeling, sir? I have heard from Charles that you do not have any recollection of arriving at Netherfield. Is that true?" She shrieked.

Darcy took a deep breath. He had been feeling better and was pleased to be out of his rooms finally but his headache returned as soon as Miss

Bingley entered with all her perfumery and screeching voice.

"I am well enough now, although my headache is returning. It is true that I do not have any memory of those few days but everything else seems to be working well." Darcy brusquely answered. He had little tolerance for this woman entering his private space.

Richard had taken Georgiana to Longhorn or Longbottom Lodge or something rather, to pay call on the new love of his life, and Bingley had gone with them. He had ventured downstairs to the library and had been peacefully engulfed in the last chapter of *The Tempest* to read the ending once again when he had been interrupted.

Darcy began to stand to leave the room, seeing that Miss Bingley had closed the door on her way in.

"Please do not leave, Fitzwilliam." Miss Bingley spoke. "We have several items to discuss."

Darcy was shocked at the familiarity that she was using and opened his mouth to scold her but she continued to speak.

"You have forgotten that you proposed to me, my dear, and my heart is broken. Do you not remember it? You gave me your mother's ring with your proposal." She lifted her hand to show him the familiar ring on her finger. "You arrived at Netherfield and that very night, you sought a private time with me and begged me to marry you. We… You told me that you loved me so much… and we… we anticipated our vows that very night. I… You asked me… you wished me to join you in your rooms… and I gave you… you took my virtue a fortnight ago, Fitzwilliam. Then you had your accident and I had to suffer without being able to see you or care for my betrothed and I could tell no one all this time, as we had not told anyone of our engagement yet, and you… and we did not tell Charles of our love for each other. I was so miserable waiting for you to declare yourself." She wiped her non-existent tears with her handkerchief. "We must tell everyone now. We must make our engagement public."

"NO!" Darcy shouted. *What is she saying? That I begged her for marriage and took her to my bed? Am I the crazy one or is she? There is no way in hell I would propose to her!*

"Miss Bingley, I may not have any memory of the past week but I have serious doubt that I proposed to you, madam." He began, but was quickly interrupted by her shrill voice.

"ARE YOU CALLING ME A LIAR?!" Caroline shouted. "How DARE you, sir? I have proof on my hand. You gave me this ring!"

Darcy stepped away and faced the window to think. *How in the world does she have Mother's ring? It is an heirloom and it definitely looks like Mother's. How could I have given it to her? I do not recall even having it in my possession. I think I last saw it at Pemberley.*

He quickly found an excuse. "I apologize if I was ungentlemanly to accuse you. I have no memory and ask you to excuse me, Miss Bingley." *I must investigate further before I risk my reputation to jilt her. I would never commit to this shrew for life!* "Since I do not remember, we must wait until my memory returns. No one knows of our engagement and we must keep it private until I am able to remember."

He turned and saw Miss Bingley's pale face. *I believe she is lying to me. She is a liar and is trying to entrap me somehow but I need proof!*

"But, but... what if your memory never returns? How much longer must I keep the happiest news of my life a secret?" Miss Bingley spat.

Darcy sneered, "You must have told your dear sister, whom you always praise as being the best of friend you could ever have."

Caroline turned bright red, "Of course not! Louisa does not know about our betrothal nor does she know of our incredible night together. Do you remember what I wore, Fitzwilliam? My sheer gown that you tore off me as you ravaged me." She drew closer to where Darcy was standing and began to lower her dress down to expose her shoulder. "You made love to me for hours and told me that I was the best you had ever had."

"Now I KNOW you are a liar, Miss Bingley!" Darcy turned and walked briskly away from her, opening the library door for propriety, and exploded in fury. "There is no way that you would hold such a *significant* event from your sister, first of all, and I would never commit such a dishonorable act, to ruin a maiden before my vows. If I truly proposed to you, the whole of London would know of it already, as I have NEVER seen you keep your mouth closed for longer than it takes for you to chew your food. Colonel Fitzwilliam has told me that you have begun to tell your neighbors here that we have an understanding and nothing could be further from the truth. I find nothing pleasing about you. Your teeth are tolerable but I do not perceive anything extraordinary about you. You have a sharp shrewish look and I would never, in a million years, consider you suitable to be Mistress of Pemberley."

Caroline fumed. "Well, I have proof on my finger that you proposed to me and your lack of memory does not change anything. I will tell everyone that you took my virtue and that you are the worst of rakes!"

Darcy laughed out at this. "And your reputation will be the only thing ruined then, Miss Bingley. I will find out the truth and once I have my proof of your lies, I will make sure you get what you deserve. My good opinion, once lost, is lost forever, madam."

He left the room without bowing to her and returned to his rooms. He was seething in anger but did not know how he would prove her lies.

I do not wish for my reputation to be damaged but I know she has lied about everything. There is no way in hell that I would propose to her; and to sleep with her, impossible!

He called out for his valet.

"Yes, Mr. Darcy." Wilkins answered as he entered.

"Wilkins, can you tell me if Miss Bingley has been trying to compromise me?" Darcy asked bluntly.

Wilkins, ever impassive, calmly answered, "But of course, sir. Since the first night of your arrival, she has attempted to enter your rooms. She was successful the very first night, as we did not realize she already had the key to this room, and you called out for me to enter your rooms to evict her out of here."

"And was she wearing a pink nightgown?" Darcy carefully asked.

Wilkins smiled, "Yes, sir. It was a hideous pink with feathers sticking out and it made her look like a dead bird. You told me that she made you nauseous."

Darcy laughed uncontrollably for a moment. "I remember that." He froze. "I remember it! You grabbed her arm to pull her out and she shouted something like, 'Get your filthy hands off me, you lout!' and you told her something about your hands being clean."

Wilkins chuckled softly. "Yes, sir. I told her I had just washed my hands so they were not filthy."

"And she has been attempting to enter every night?" Darcy probed.

"Yes, sir. Colonel Fitzwilliam and I have been vigilant in ensuring that you recover without her disruptions and someone has always been with you, either myself or Miss Darcy or the colonel, for your protection." Wilkins answered.

Darcy released a breath of relief as he looked out the window. "Thank you, Wilkins. I appreciate your diligence more than you know. Doctor Hastings has given me permission to resume my normal activities in a day or two and I hope to return home. I will not stay here with Miss Bingley under the same roof. Wilkins," he turned to face his valet again, "do you know anything about my mother's ring? The one with the sapphire center and pearls around it? Miss Bingley has it and is fabricating a story that I gave it to her with a proposal of marriage. I do not have any recollection of it."

"I am sorry, sir. I do not know anything about it." Wilkins answered. He paused before he continued, "But there is something else..."

"What is it, my man?" Darcy asked.

Wilkins pulled out a small cloth from his coat pocket. "After your injury, I cleaned your clothes and found this in the waistcoat pocket. It was soaked in blood and I washed it but then saw that it did not belong to you. I do not know where it is from but it appears someone assisted you during your injury." He handed the item to Darcy.

"Thank you, Wilkins. You may return to your duties." Darcy dismissed his faithful valet and sat on a chair to look at the delicate handkerchief in his hand. There were still bloodstains that could not be washed out, but on one corner, it was embroidered with a feminine stitching of Sweet William flowers.

Lizzy! This was Lizzy's! Darcy remembered. He saw her eyes again. *Who is she?*

Chapter 5

"I knew you could not be so beautiful for nothing, Jane!" Mrs. Bennet screeched. "Mr. Bingley is positively smitten with you. And you, Lizzy, Colonel Fitzwilliam is already in love with you, I think. He brought his cousin already to introduce you!"

"Oh, mama, although I agree that Mr. Bingley is half in love with Jane already, Colonel Fitzwilliam brought his cousin so he could introduce her to me. He had already shared with me yesterday that he wished his cousin to meet ladies closer to her age, as she is not yet out and does not know anyone here." Elizabeth answered.

Mrs. Bennet nodded. "Yes, what fine dress she wore. Such elegant materials, even if there was a lack of lace. Your Aunt Philips told me that Miss Darcy's brother is worth 10,000 a year. Can you imagine such a sum? 10,000 a year! If only he had attended the assembly, he would have noted Jane and swooped her up right away. But Mr. Bingley will do. Jane will capture him and perhaps your befriending Miss Darcy will help you capture her brother. Even if he is not interested in your wild ways, he may throw you and your sisters in the path of his rich friends."

Elizabeth laughed, "Well, I have it on good authority that Mr. Darcy would find me ghastly, so I will have to be a doting aunt to Jane's dozen children and be an old maid." She winked at her elder sister.

"Oh, Lizzy, stuff and nonsense. You are quite pretty, even if not as much as Jane." Mrs. Bennet shook her handkerchief at her. "I believe Miss Darcy liked all of us quite well. She was shy but very well-mannered. Very much a lady."

Lizzy suddenly had a bright idea. "You know, mama, she is from the first circles. Colonel Fitzwilliam shared with me that he is the second son of an earl, and that Mr. and Miss Darcy are not only extremely wealthy but their grandfather was an earl. Do you know anyone else who is of the first circles? It is extraordinary to befriend one, as you know."

Mrs. Bennet contemplated her second daughter's question. "Well, Mr. Bingley and his sisters must certainly…"

"No, mama. Mr. Bingley is the son of a tradesman. Although very wealthy, he might be of the second or third circles at best, as he is not yet a landowner. To be acquaintances of the first circles is a great privilege and we must not bring shame to Jane, right, mama?" Elizabeth planted a seed in her mother's mind. She did not like to resort to such schemes but for her dearest sister's happiness, she would do anything for her.

"How would we bring shame? What are you speaking of?" Mrs. Bennet panicked.

"Well, you saw how Miss Bingley and Mrs. Hurst looked down at us, did you not, mama? They witnessed Kitty and Lydia dancing and loudly laughing and running around like children at the assembly last night. I know you think them lively and happy but you saw how Miss Darcy behaved today. That is the expectation of society where Mr. Bingley inhabits, and my sisters' behaviors are not appropriate in their circles. Miss Darcy appeared quite shy and she definitely preferred Jane and my company over Lydia's, who is closest in age." Lizzy poked a little harder. "Learning that Lydia was out at fifteen was shocking to Miss Darcy and even Colonel Fitzwilliam appeared quite appalled with her flirtations. Kitty followed right along and you saw how he wanted nothing to do with them."

Mrs. Bennet shrieked, "You are right! Lydia! Kitty! How could you? Do not dare ruin Jane's chance of capturing Mr. Bingley!" She began to squeal, "My salts! Get my smelling salts!"

Jane quietly stood and fetched the smelling salts and handed it to her mother.

Mrs. Bennet bemoaned, "Oh, my nerves! How will I handle living in the hedgerows if Mr. Bennet should die and leave us all destitute? Oh, you do not know what I suffer! I have such trembling, such fluttering, such spasms in my side..."

"What is all this ruckus?" Mr. Bennet boomed at the door.

"Oh, Mr. Bennet! We are all in an uproar! Jane is going to be jilted by Mr. Bingley because he is not of the first class and Lydia and Kitty will drive him away! They are nothing to Miss Darcy and even Colonel Fitzwilliam was disgusted. We will all be thrown into the hedgerows!" She wailed.

Mr. Bennet lifted his eyebrow at Elizabeth in query and Elizabeth suppressed a giggle while winking at her father.

Mr. Bennet sat next to his wife and patted her hand rather condescendingly. "There, there, Mrs. Bennet. Perhaps I will outlive you and you will not be left in the hedgerows." He teased. Mrs. Bennet bawled even louder with this and Mr. Bennet chuckled softly. "Are you telling me that Lydia and Kitty need to be reined in a little?" He surmised.

"NO! Papa! Mama is wrong. We would never shame Jane. Mama always told us that we were exciting and brought everyone so much joy. You cannot punish us for being so cheerful!" Lydia whined and crossed her arms in anger.

Kitty, seeing her younger sister upset, followed her action as usual and crossed her arms and huffed as well.

"I am almost sad to have missed the assembly last night. Almost. My dear Mrs. Bennet, I will support you in any regulations you wish for our youngest two daughters, as I am certain Jane has comported herself well, my Lizzy can discern for herself, and Mary can do no wrong since she is so obliging. If you should like to place the girls back in the nursery," he heard his two youngest daughters begin to sob, "I will agree with you, since they will embarrass Jane and her already planned marriage to a man she met only last night." Mr. Bennet jeered.

Elizabeth rolled her eyes with her father's tease. She understood her father better than anyone and knew he would press too far if she allowed it. She saw Jane comfort Lydia and Kitty and spoke when the room quieted further.

"Papa, I believe mama is concerned that my youngest sisters do not know some of the rules of society and as we have not had a governess to teach us of such things, they just need to be better-guided." She saw Lydia and Kitty's face snap to attention. "Aunt Madeline has been a great help to Jane and me and some to Mary. Mary had been willing to listen to what Jane and I had learned but Kitty and Lydia have not. Although I do believe being out at fifteen is too young, I believe that if my sisters can take Miss Darcy as an example of how a young lady should behave in public, they will grow to be fine ladies and capture themselves very eligible suitors like Jane." She winked at her father discreetly. "She invited us to call on her tomorrow at Netherfield and perhaps Kitty and Lydia can begin their lessons immediately with Jane and myself today."

Mrs. Bennet sat up abruptly, "That is an excellent idea, Lizzy! Girls," she pointed at Kitty and Lydia, "you will sit with your sisters and take notes. You will learn to be proper ladies like the first circles and behave like Miss Darcy. Miss Bingley was very stuck-up and of course it is because she is of the *third* circles. I liked Mr. Bingley very well, of course, but his sisters, it is obvious they are lower by the way they behave. Yes, that is a good idea. And if you do not take the time to learn, I *will* put you back in the nursery, girls!" She threatened.

Having never had their mother chastise them for their liveliness before, Kitty and Lydia were afraid of the retribution of disobeying her and nodded their heads quickly in agreement.

Jane leaned over to Elizabeth and whispered, "What have you done, Lizzy? I appreciate that you are attempting to rein in our sisters but you do realize that we will actually have to spend more time with them? And how difficult it will be to hear them whine?" She winked at her dear sister.

Elizabeth giggled as she covered her mouth with her hand. "Oh, Jane, if only for your happiness, I am willing to suffer our coarse sisters to educate them. They have been without guidance for too long."

"Well then, Mrs. Bennet, I will leave you to them." Mr. Bennet spoke as he stood. "Lizzy, will you join me in the study?"

"Of course, father." Elizabeth smiled and walked with him.

~~*~*~*~*

"Lizzy, I trust you will take care of matters with your sisters. I am pleased to hear that your mother is willing to have them educated a little more. I liked how Mrs. Annesley was guiding Miss Darcy out of her shyness. Perhaps you might see if that lady is willing to oversee your sisters a little. I can offer a small reward for her assistance." Mr. Bennet commented.

Elizabeth pulled out a coin and placed it on her father's desk. "I have a guinea here to help out. Any education my sisters receive will be worth the cost."

Mr. Bennet reached for the coin and looked at it closely. "Ah, your payment for helping out Mr. Darcy. Who would have believed his sister would call on us today." He looked at her daughter discreetly to see a blush on her cheeks. "This gentleman that you helped, what did you think of him?"

"Oh, papa, he was very handsome but you heard what is being said about him. Mr. Darcy is worth at least 10,000 a year and he is nephew to an earl. He thought I was monstrous and I was offended but I know his head was addled so I forgive him, but then he gave me that coin thinking that I was a servant and continued to insult me thoroughly. It is no wonder he thought me so low, learning that he is so high in society. The way he spoke to me, the way he behaved, I can see him being a proud, arrogant man." She replied.

"As I have not met the man and since his head was knocked about when you met him, I will reserve my opinions until I can actually observe him." He returned the coin back to his favorite daughter. "Your reward is yours to keep. Perhaps you may add it to your dowry." He teased.

Elizabeth laughed, "'A penny spared is twice got.' It is a good proverb by George Herbert, papa."

"Have you finished your copy of *La Belle et la Bête*? I just finished its translation in English if you would like to read it next." Mr. Bennet changed the topic.

Elizabeth smiled broadly. "Almost, papa. I would love to read *Beauty and the Beast* and see if my translations are correct. It is a very enjoyable story."

"Whenever you are ready, child." Mr. Bennet nodded and grinned at his favorite child. "Perhaps you should make it a requirement for the girls to read and learn some languages as well. You are proficient in French and Italian. Perhaps a little German?" He winked as he returned to his books.

Chapter 6

Darcy smiled as he listened to Georgiana speak faster and more energetically than she had in months. He truly did not care too much for all the ladies she met today but Richard had been right that she needed acquaintances nearer her age.

"...and Miss Elizabeth was so kind. Of the five sisters, I liked her best because she made me laugh." Georgiana continued speaking.

"Five sisters in one family? No brothers?" Darcy asked.

"No, no brothers. Were you not listening? Five daughters, the estate is entailed to a distant cousin, a Mr. Callings or something, who would own the stool of the pianoforte, according to Miss Mary. Miss Kitty and Lydia were very loud and they were flirting with Richard but..."

"And how did Richard take that? I thought he was in love with Miss Bennet." Darcy interrupted.

Georgiana giggled, "No, no, William! Mr. Bingley is in love with Miss Bennet, Jane Bennet, and Richard is in love with... well, I think he is trying to matchmake *you* with Miss Elizabeth. I have to agree with him. I think

Miss Elizabeth would be a great sister... I mean, wife for you." She blushed, "Oh, William, I would love to have a sister like her. She made me feel at ease and she joked with Richard and even scolded him when he asked questions that were too personal. But her manners were a mixture of sweetness and archness that it would make it difficult to affront anybody, and she is so witty. I asked all the Miss Bennets to call on me tomorrow; I hope it will be acceptable to you. Miss Bingley did tell me to treat her home like my own and Mr. Bingley dearly wished it as well."

Darcy's mood darkened, as he remembered what Caroline Bingley was attempting to do. *If I could quickly get engaged to a woman of some means, Caroline Bingley would be considered jilted without damage to my reputation. But who? If Lizzy was real, if she were not so frightening in appearance, if, if...*

"Are you well, William?" Georgiana asked when she saw Darcy in deep thought with his brows furrowed. "Your headache, has it returned?"

Darcy immediately straightened and put on a pleasanter face. "No, no, sweetling. I am well. My mind just drifted, that is all."

Georgiana smiled in relief. "I will get dressed for dinner, then. I am very excited for the next few days, William. I will see Miss Elizabeth tomorrow here and at Lucas Lodge for dinner the day after. Thank you for agreeing to take me. You are the best of brothers!" She kissed his cheek and left.

Darcy had decided to not burden his sister with Caroline Bingley's attempt at entrapment. That mercenary woman would not risk her reputation by exposing her loss of virtue, and he would find a way to get himself untangled. He would talk to Richard and Bingley and see what could be done. He trusted his cousin and his friend with his life and he had told Bingley numerous times before that he would never consider Miss Bingley for a wife, no matter how much she attempted to compromise him, so he knew he could go to his friend with this concern. Darcy had wished to depart for Pemberley in the next day or two but with Georgiana befriending the Bennet sisters, he felt guilty to pull her away from her newfound companions.

~~*~*~*~*

"There you are, Darcy!" Richard smiled after knocking on the library door and entering. "I thought you would be locked up in your rooms to avoid Miss Bingley."

"Richard, I do not avoid anyone. I refuse to be imprisoned in my rooms when I am the guest. But I am done with that woman." Darcy bitterly retorted.

"Now what as she done?" Richard asked.

Just then, there was another knock on the door. Bingley entered with his face red, appearing quite angry, which was completely opposite of his usual joviality.

"And what has happened to you, Bingley? I just left you to change for dinner." Richard exclaimed.

"My sister, that is what happened. I am so... aargh! Why could my sister not be like your sister, Darcy? Caroline is the most awful harridan and I cannot stand her!" Bingley replied.

"It sounds like both of you are angry with the same person. Explain. Bingley, you first." Richard commanded.

Bingley stroked his fingers through his hair. "Caroline demanded that we return to London immediately and that guests or not, we should all depart back to town and leave this 'god-forsaken backwater country' and all its peasant residents who have nothing to offer to raise our status. She said that she was already tired of being here and desired for better company in town. She told me that Darcy here," pointing to his friend, "treated her most abominably, and that she was most ill-used. She would not tell me anything else but I have a feeling she is trying to trick me into something. She said that Jane Bennet was tolerable but would do nothing to raise our status and that I should pursue Miss Darcy. She told me that I should corner your sister and compromise her into marrying me! My sister, who professes to be such an accomplished lady, told me to compromise a sixteen-year-old girl! I have never heard such nonsense. I told her that she could leave by herself but she told me that she would force Louisa to leave with her and there would be no hostess here for me to be able to entertain. And of course Louisa took her side, as always. What in hell is wrong with her? Both of my sisters?"

Richard shook his head in disgust. *I already knew Caroline Bingley was a harpy but I cannot believe how awful she could be. I would have killed Bingley with my bare hands if he attempted to ruin Georgie.*

"And what about you, Darcy? What has Miss Bingley done to you?" Richard asked calmly.

Darcy took a deep breath and took a sip of his brandy. "Apparently, Miss Bingley told me that as soon as I stepped foot into Netherfield last week, I professed my undying love for her and begged her to marry me. She showed me my mother's ring on her hand and told me that it was proof of our betrothal and... Bingley, she told me... she accused me of bringing her into my bed to anticipate our vows. All this apparently happened my first night of arrival and right before my accident."

"And how convenient it is that you have no memory of that time and Miss Bingley would readily supply you with such a dramatic version as soon as she found out you could not remember." Richard scoffed.

Bingley poured himself a large glass of alcohol and gulped it down. "She is an awful, mercenary shrew and I never thought she would take it so far. I believe you, my friend. You have told me time and time again that you would never marry her and for you to suddenly arrive and propose marriage is ridiculous. You... you did not," he poured another glass and sipped it this time, "you did not actually take her to..."

"Of course not, Bingley! Do you honestly believe me capable of doing such a thing? You know I have... limited experience and for my firs... it would never be with your sister, of all people!" Darcy proclaimed.

Bingley looked relieved. Darcy continued, "Wilkins told me that he arrived in time to see her dressed in an atrocious nightgown and promptly kicked her out of my rooms. I remember bits of it as well, and no, she was not near my bed. Richard here," he looked at his favorite cousin, "has been vigilant along with my valet, and I have been kept safe. I have been trying to put all the pieces together and I have discovered that I must have been angry that morning because of her attempt, but I do not know how I could have had the accident nor do I understand some of the flashes of memory that I see. I have seen monsters and I have awakened from a nightmare of my horse appearing an absolutely gruesome beast. I do not understand it. I saw another creature," he eyed Richard, "with freckles and warts who appeared heinous but was kind to me to help me with my injury. I do not understand it at all."

Richard scribbled some notes onto a small notebook then he leaned in curiously to the book that was sitting next to Darcy and reached for it. "Darcy, were you reading this book before arriving at Hertfordshire?"

Darcy saw the cover and nodded. "I had just finished it recently and had begun another. It was sitting here so I was looking at it again. Why?"

Richard began to laugh. "I know no one thinks I actually read, but I do like books, Darcy. This is *The Tempest*. Do you remember who one of the main characters in this play is? Caliban."

Darcy sat for a moment and as understanding dawned, his mouth gaped opened.

"What does that mean? Who is Caliban?" Bingley asked. "I have not read it. You both may read quite a bit but I skipped this one. Who is Caliban?"

Darcy slowly nodded. "Yes, Caliban. He is an ugly creature, son of a witch, who is described to be freckled and hideous. He is written to be grotesque in appearance and it must be what my mind had formed after my accident. How is it possible for me to imagine such a thing?" Darcy sat in deep thought. *Perhaps my Lizzy is not so heinous after all. Perhaps I imagined everything after I hit my head.* He fingered the handkerchief in his waistcoat pocket. *She was real. I did not imagine her, she is real.*

"So your monster wif... rescuer was imaged after Caliban and might not be a beastly creature. What did you begin to read after?" Richard inquired.

"I began to read *Beauty and the Beast*. I had finished it in English and wished to start it in French, in its original version." Darcy answered.

Richard laughed. "Too many monsters and beasts! Perhaps you should read more poetry, Darcy. No wonder your nightmares are filled with such frightful scenes."

Darcy smiled. "Yes, Richard. Perhaps more poetry for me. Maybe love poems."

Bingley laughed, returning to more of his jovial self. "Or you can be like me and not read at all. My dreams are filled with lovely ladies and dancing." He sobered quickly, thinking of entertaining, "What am I to do with Caroline? What can I do without a hostess?"

Richard laughed loudly. "Well, the role of a hostess is to be female and order the servants about; that is what your sister does, does she not?" The other two men chuckled as well. "You have forgotten that you have the current Mistress of Pemberley residing under your roof. Georgiana may not be out yet but she is more than capable of inviting a few ladies over and handling dinner menus. She has learned much from my mother, the Countess of Matlock, and is fully capable of being your hostess for the remainder of our stay. Perhaps if you tell Miss Bingley how insignificant her threats are, she will cease to be such a pain in your ass! Make her plan a Ball. Make her miserable and invite a hundred of your neighbors here!"

Darcy grumbled, "But I would rather she be gone. What do I do about her threat to me, Richard? She said she would ruin my reputation if I do not marry her. She is insistent that I have taken her virtue and that my mother's ring is proof of our betrothal. I cannot recall, and Wilkins does not know either, how in the world that ring ended up on her finger. Unless she has had it faked somewhere, it is my mother's ring and I cannot comprehend it."

"Why not ask Georgie? Perhaps she showed it to Miss Bingley and it was replicated somehow, or... I hate to say it, Bingley... but it might have been stolen from Pemberley." Richard commented.

Bingley groaned, "Aargh... if she has stolen it from you, Darcy, she could be hanged. She would bring shame to my family and I would kill her myself."

"My mother's ring, if it is indeed authentic, is priceless, as it is believed to have been once owned by Queen Elizabeth herself. I do not understand how it could have ended up with Miss Bingley when it was last in Pemberley's safe." Darcy stated. "I do not wish to have Georgie involved yet. She is so happy here. I have not seen her so delighted to make new acquaintances and I do not wish to disrupt her peace yet. I know she will feel guilty if Miss Bingley had stolen it from Pemberley or if I ask her to leave Netherfield because of a pending scandal. I wish to keep my baby sister protected a little while longer." He sighed.

Richard tapped his shoulder. "I understand, Darcy. Although I think you should tell Georgiana everything, I know you wish to keep her untarnished from the evils of the world for as long as possible. She is growing up to be a fine lady, Darcy. I know she could handle it but I sympathize with you as well." He smiled. "It is dinnertime. Perhaps we can make Miss Bingley as uncomfortable as much as possible and she will retire to her rooms for the next," he pulled out his pocket watch, "fortnight?"

They laughed and with a lighter heart, joined the others for dinner.

Chapter 7

"Madam," he bowed, "Madam," he bowed again, he bowed three more times, as the ladies were introduced, barely looking at their skirts and avoiding eye contact. Darcy rolled his eyes behind Bingley's back as his friend was gushing at the fair-haired lady who spoke quietly. She was as beautiful as Bingley had described, tall and willowy in frame, who appeared as serene as one could be. His friend had a particular preference and it was always the same. Same height, same figure, same hair, same dullness. Darcy could not understand why Bingley would be so interested in someone who looked so much like every lady before, even if this Miss Bennet was a little prettier in the face than the other dozen women Bingley had fancied.

He looked around and saw Georgiana already in rapid conversation with a dark-haired woman. *The second daughter, I think.* Darcy thought. He could not see her face, as that lady was facing away from him, with two other younger girls sitting and observing Georgiana carefully. *The fourth and fifth daughters.*

Darcy saw the third Miss Bennet sitting next to Miss Jane Bennet. *Mary Bennet.* He attempted to remember all of their names. He had never paid attention to single ladies if he could help it, and having five intrude all at the same time was overwhelming. *Elizabeth is the one that Georgiana favors.* He remembered. *The other two, Cathy? Libby?*

He chuckled softly as he watched Richard practically drooling over Miss Elizabeth. Darcy had taken his place nearer to Bingley and still could not get a good look at Miss Elizabeth. *I thought Richard had already given up on Miss Elizabeth. His future wife, how laughable. These ladies, if I can judge by their dresses, are not well off at all. Miss Bingley and Mrs. Hurst's dresses are horrid but their materials are by far more expensive. This Miss Elizabeth would be a terrible wife to Richard and she would never qualify as Mrs. Darcy with her relatives in trade and no dowry.*

Darcy was in deep thought. He looked over at Miss Bingley and Mrs. Hurst, who were exchanging pleasantries with Miss Bennet. Darcy knew that Bingley had threatened his sisters with what they feared most: Financial penalty.

Bingley had told Caroline that if she stepped one toe out of line, if she decided to leave Netherfield, or to cause Darcy any more trouble, he would require her to pay him back for all of the years of overspending and would be banned from his homes, here in Hertfordshire as well as the

London townhouse.

The Hursts, who did not have a home in London, would also be evicted, and for the first time in their four-year marriage, Mr. Hurst put his foot down and commanded his wife to obey his brother's wishes. Mr. Hurst's family home was located in a desolate town, ten miles north of Liverpool, and he had hated being there with nothing to do and a serious lack of good wine.

Miss Bingley had apologized to Darcy and promised that she would not spread any word of their engagement. She refused to return the ring, though, still holding firm that once his memories returned, they would be married and she would hold on to the proof of their betrothal.

Darcy still did not have any proof of the theft or deception so he had let it go for now. Suddenly, his hearing snapped to attention when he heard his sister utter the next words.

"Lizzy! You must come and visit me at Pemberley! You must promise me, Lizzy!" Georgiana cried.

Lizzy! Miss Elizabeth is Lizzy? Darcy's eyes opened wide. He stood immediately and without another thought, he walked over to where Miss Elizabeth was sitting. He stood behind her, half hoping she was *his* Lizzy, half wishing she was not, unsure of what to say or what to expect. *I just need to see her eyes. I need to see if she is the one I have been dreaming of.*

"Brother! Please say yes! I have been telling Lizzy about Pemberley and she had always wished to visit Lambton. Lizzy usually goes to London after Christmas but perhaps she can come visit me if her father agrees. Please say yes." Georgiana begged, seeing Darcy stand behind Miss Elizabeth.

Darcy smiled softly at his sister's excitement. "Of course, Georgiana. As you wish." His heart thumped louder as Miss Elizabeth began to turn to face him. "Miss Elizabeth, it would be an honor to host..." He met her eyes and froze. It was the same pair of sparkling eyes that had invaded his thoughts day and night.

Elizabeth smiled slightly, seeing the handsome gentleman finally look at her. She had avoided facing him fully in fear that he might continue to find her horrendous and she flushed now, realizing that he was still shocked to see her as an awful monster.

"Oh, Georgiana, I am afraid I offend your brother with my appearance. We will talk of my trip later. Will you show me a dressing room? I would like to refresh myself." Elizabeth quickly asked.

Georgiana was quite confused but stood and walked her dear friend for privacy, who insisted she did not require assistance, and returned to continue her conversation with Kitty and Lydia, who were asking several questions demurely today, and she had begun to enjoy their company more. She glanced at her brother whose face was stern, as she had often seen when his headaches had pained him.

Richard, who had been speaking with the two younger ladies, finding them more pleasant without the crass flirtations, saw Darcy still standing still behind the couch and became concerned. He seemed perfectly fine until he interrupted Georgiana's conversation with Miss Elizabeth and while Miss Elizabeth paled and left for the dressing room, Darcy had remained in the same place without moving. He winked at Georgiana to communicate with her silently and stood. He approached Darcy, discreetly pulling him to a corner to look out the window. "Are you well, Darcy? Is it your head?"

Darcy startled, "Yes. Yes, it is my head. I need to rest. Make some excuse for me. I must go." And without acknowledging anyone in the room, he quickly rushed out of the room.

Richard put on a false smile, "Darcy needs to see to something in his rooms. He will return as soon as he can." He returned to the ladies and continued to converse, and although concerned for his cousin, he knew Darcy required privacy to rest.

~~*~*~*~*

Elizabeth looked at herself in the mirror. She saw nothing out of order, she thought she looked quite well today. She wiped away the tears that had fallen and pinched her cheeks to give it some color.

After befriending Georgiana Darcy and realizing that the Mr. Darcy who had suffered the fall from his horse was actually Miss Darcy's brother, she had been nervous and eager to see the handsome gentleman again. She had been quite insulted that he thought her so hideous, but as he had been seeing monsters, she had hoped that he had found her at least tolerable now. When she finally met his eyes and his face turned into a fierce look, as if he still found her loathsome and hateful, her vanity had been crushed and she could not remain composed in the same room.

Well, fine! If he hates my appearance that much, I will never see him again. As long as Jane is happy with Mr. Bingley and he does not disrupt their peace, I will only befriend Georgiana and be out of his sight as much as possible. I will not let him affect me so! She determined.

Straightening her posture and ready to face the world again, she stepped out of the small room to return to the party.

"Lizzy! It is you!" Darcy walked briskly towards her as soon as she exited, and he grabbed her by her upper arm to practically drag her into the library.

Darcy quickly closed the door and held her face with both hands, cradling both of her cheeks and looking into her eyes as if inspecting a horse for sale.

"What are you doing? Mr. Darcy, release me immediately!" Elizabeth scowled.

Darcy ignored her pleas. He drew closer to her, his chest almost touching hers. "It is you, Lizzy? My monster? My loathsome creature with the beautiful eyes? My Lizzy?" He continued to ask. "Did you or did you not help me after I fell from my horse?"

Elizabeth could only nod once and his lips were on hers as soon as she confirmed his answer.

Darcy kissed her lips roughly and pressed his body against hers. He needed to connect with her; he wanted to touch her and make sure she was real. He had dreamt of her for over a fortnight and could not believe that he was holding her in his arms again. His need to taste her grew and he delved his tongue in her mouth to reach her deeper; to attach himself to her somehow, to join with her, wishing to make her his own.

Elizabeth was completely bewildered. This man had yelled at her, insulted her several times, held her in his arms, showed his disgust in company, and now was ardently kissing her. She thought of slapping him but as his passion grew, she succumbed to his fervor and returned his kisses.

But when his hand traveled down and he pressed his hand onto her buttocks to press against his body, she felt a protrusion against her stomach and jumped, realizing that she was being compromised.

She pushed him away from her as far as possible and slapped him across the cheek.

In shock, Darcy yelled out, "Why did you do that for?"

Elizabeth fumed. "First you yell and insult me, now you force your kiss onto me like a rake, and you ask me why I slapped you? I know you still think me a loathsome creature. Why did you kiss me? Am I some game to you? Now that you know I am not a servant, am I no longer safe from you?" She scoffed. "I saw the look in your eyes. You still find me horrid and yet I attract you enough for you to use me for your pleasures?"

Darcy realized his mistake once again. He had never acted so irrationally before but finally meeting her and seeing that she was not just an apparition had been a shock. She was beautiful. *His* Lizzy was absolutely stunning in her face, in her figure, especially her eyes.

"I am sorry, Lizzy. I have never behaved so impulsively before, but I was stunned to see you. I have had a memory loss and I do not recall what happened to cause my accident but I remembered you. I remembered bits of you but mostly your eyes and your kindness." He drew close to her very slowly so that he did not frighten her or get another slap in the face. "You are so beautiful, Lizzy. More beautiful than I ever imagined. Even when I visualized you to be a loathsome monster, I loved you. I fell in love with your kind heart and I could not stop thinking of you." He cradled her cheek like he had done the first time he met her. "You have a beautiful soul and you have captured my heart." He leaned closer and gently kissed her lips again.

Elizabeth closed her eyes and reveled in his declaration but was alerted to reality when she heard Georgiana's voice in the hallway, calling out her name.

She jumped back a step and looked at the gentleman. "You cannot love me; you do not know me. You know nothing about me and I do not know anything about you. For you to declare your love is ridiculous and you are a rake for all I know. Please, do not do this again."

Elizabeth quickly turned and opened the door, closing it behind her to keep him inside the library.

"Dear Georgiana, I took a wrong turn. Thank you for coming to my rescue. Let us return to the others." She quickly grabbed her friend's arm and led her back to the sitting room.

Darcy stood against the door with his forehead resting on it. *What have I done? I have never kissed a woman like that before. I know it is astonishing but I love her. I love Elizabeth Bennet and she thinks me a rake because I behaved like a rake. I assaulted her and considered taking her virtue right here, right now. My God, Richard was right. I need to make Elizabeth Bennet my wife. But how?*

His head was indeed throbbing now. He quietly opened the door to see no one about and sprinted to his rooms.

He lay on his bed and pulled out the bloodstained handkerchief that he had always carried. *Elizabeth Bennet is my Lizzy! My beastly creature; no, my beautiful Lizzy, my pretty, witty, gorgeous, sensual Lizzy. I must have her know me better and make her mine. I have thought of no one, nothing else since meeting her and this was when I thought her a deformed monster. I need her. How do I make her love me?*

His head pierced and he closed his eyes. He placed her handkerchief over his eyes and remembered her face. Her eyes were always clear but now, he could see the rest of her face with a handsome nose and soft pink lips. He could taste her again in his mind and his desires grew once more. *I must make her my wife. No one else will do. I know so much more about her than she believes. She just needs to know me.* Before he could think further, he fell asleep and dreamt of his wife and future children, and he slept more peacefully than he had in months.

Chapter 8

"Miss Elizabeth Bennet." Darcy stated.

"Miss Elizabeth Bennet!" repeated Miss Bingley. "I am all astonishment. How long has she been such a favorite? And pray, when am I to wish you joy? Did you not meet her and her 'fine eyes' only yesterday?"

"It is none of your business, Miss Bingley. I refuse to discuss any more of my personal thoughts with you. Why are you here? You should not be wearing that in public." Darcy seethed, seeing his mother's ring on her hand.

"Well, Charles is forcing me to acquaint myself with these… *commoners* here and demanded that I present myself to my best advantage. Do you not agree that my dress outshines every single one of these drab ladies here? It is so obvious that they are so below us. I do not understand why my brother feels the need to be so accommodating." She huffed. "And of course this is the best jewelry that has been *gifted* to me, so I proudly wear it. Oh, if only you would remember so I can tell the whole world that I will be Mrs. Darcy."

"Never, madam. *Over my dead body."* Darcy quietly whispered. He quickly walked away from the vulgar woman and looked out the window.

He had been frustrated that Miss Elizabeth had been avoiding him all night. Whenever he drew near her, she would depart for another part of the room, and if she was stationary and in conversation, she did not speak to him and found an excuse to leave.

"Mr. Darcy," his reverie was interrupted when Mr. Bennet approached him.

"Mr. Bennet." Darcy acknowledged.

Mr. Bennet kindly smiled at the young man, noticing that he seemed to be chasing his daughter and that same daughter was avidly avoiding him. "I understand you have been recovering from a horse fall. All is well now?"

Darcy cleared his throat and straightened, realizing that this was his future father-in-law if everything went according to his wishes. "Yes, sir. I am fine now. Although I have a memory loss of two days, everything else is functioning."

"Yes, I heard about the memory loss. And there was some talk of your seeing *monsters*," Mr. Bennet chuckled, seeing Darcy color. "My Lizzy was particularly amused with the event but I can see that her vanity was quite wounded. If you had only found her tolerable, she might not be so angry with you but you called her, what did she say, 'a loathsome beast'?" He laughed as Darcy turned brighter red.

"I... I do not find her loathsome. Not in the least, sir. I apologize. I did not know... I was seeing things and..." Darcy stumbled for words, not knowing how much of his heart to reveal, and being earnestly embarrassed that he could have insulted a lady in such a way.

Mr. Bennet nodded. "I understand, Mr. Darcy. You would be a fool to insult my favorite daughter. Perhaps she might be willing to accept your apology someday." He walked away after his mild chastisement, to speak with Sir Lucas and to observe his two youngest daughters behaving more composed than he had ever seen before.

Darcy stood alone, wondering how in the world he would apologize to Lizzy, when his heart stilled for a moment hearing her voice. He walked towards the music as if in a trance and leaned against the wall to see her at the pianoforte, singing a beautiful song while her fingers played. He cared nothing for her lack of dowry or connections; whether she had a single quality dress or was wearing burlap, even if she had uncles enough to fill all Cheapside, nothing else mattered to him, as he fell deeper in love with the woman of his dreams.

~~*~*~*~*

"He certainly looks at you often, Miss Eliza," Caroline Bingley taunted. "It must be to find fault, as I am confident of his love for me." She whispered to Elizabeth as they walked arm in arm in the Netherfield gardens.

Darcy sat on a bench that overlooked the walking path and as much as he attempted to behave properly, he could not stop staring at Elizabeth Bennet, even though Richard had berated him for appearing so fearsome and Georgiana begged him to find something to like about her dearest friend.

Miss Jane Bennet had been invited alone to Netherfield a few days ago by Miss Bingley and Mrs. Hurst so that they could get to know her better, but Miss Bennet had arrived sodden on horseback and had become ill. When Miss Elizabeth had arrived the morning after, Darcy knew it was his chance to court her properly but he had no idea where to begin.

He had not told a soul what had happened with Lizzy and even Richard thought Darcy was offended by her somehow. His cousin had even apologized in trying to matchmake them and pleaded with him to be civil with her.

Darcy grew green with jealousy when Richard kissed Lizzy's hand before taking his leave yesterday to return to duties in London. He watched her blush and was tempted to grab her again and kiss her senseless in public, but he knew she would not hesitate to slap him again.

He attempted to have a pleasant conversation with her but became extremely nervous and found himself unable to carry on the simplest of exchanges without sounding like a bumbling fool. Whatever he did say was remarked with a challenge or a witty retort by this fascinating woman and every topic he solicited was diverted to include Georgiana or anyone else in the room instead. He could only wish for a private moment to beg for her mercy and for her hand in marriage but he knew Lizzy would never comply.

~~*~*~*~*

"Well, I am certain he finds many faults with me, Miss Bingley. Congratulations on your engagement with that gentleman." Elizabeth was not sure what to think. Mr. Darcy, who had proclaimed his love to her only days ago seemed to be engaged already to Mr. Bingley's sister, and Caroline had confided her in private, showing off her engagement ring and telling her that it was a secret to everyone else, behaving as if they were the best of friends.

"I am most pleased that Fitzwilliam wishes me to be Mistress of Pemberley. I have been there two summers in a row. It is the grandest home I have ever seen and it makes Netherfield look like a pauper's home. As soon as he is fully recovered, we hope to set a wedding date." Caroline leaned closer and whispered quietly, "Hopefully sooner than later. I believe I am carrying his heir already." She winked.

Caroline had seen the look of lust in Mr. Darcy's eyes whenever he turned to Eliza Bennet. He had never looked at a woman like that before and she boiled with jealousy when he declared Miss Eliza's eyes to be very fine. Caroline hated that interloper, who took all of her attentions away from Mr. Darcy, who should be looking at herself. *I am the one wearing his mother's ring. I am the one that he is betrothed to, whether he likes it or not. If I can only get back into his rooms and sneak into his bed, he would have to marry me. I might have to find someone to get me pregnant so I can dupe him into believing that he truly impregnated me.*

Elizabeth nodded her head and continued her walk without speaking further. She was in shock as she thought over Caroline Bingley's words.

He is already engaged, he tried to impose on me while already promised to another, and he has already anticipated his vows. He is truly a rake. I believed him more honorable but I suppose I do not know him at all. Georgiana believes him to be the best of brothers, but oh, what secrets we keep from our own siblings. I have not told Jane of my history with Mr. Darcy and I suppose Mr. Darcy keeps many secrets from his own sister.

She sighed in disappointment. *Even though he does not speak much, what he says when he speaks is intelligent and he seems to be a good man otherwise. My first impressions were quite accurate. He is an arrogant womanizer and he probably only wishes me to warm his bed, or God forbid, be his mistress after he marries Miss Bingley. I cannot imagine him happy with her, though. She is not good enough for him.*

Elizabeth had to be honest with herself, *But he is handsome and generous. He is good to Georgiana and if he were not engaged, if he were more honorable, it would be a great privilege to be loved by him.*

She shook off her thoughts and excused herself to return to Jane's bedside.

~~*~*~*~*

Darcy growled. *Damn! She has run away once again. Why does she insist on avoiding me?* He saw Elizabeth curtsey to Miss Bingley and he walked rapidly after her but she was too quick and had run into Miss Bennet's room before he could call out to her.

He stood outside her door, scratching his head, to figure out a way to approach her again without scaring her off. Then suddenly, the door opened and he saw Lizzy exit.

Elizabeth froze when she saw him several feet away.

"Lizzy," Darcy began. "I need to speak with you. I must apologize and I wish to clear the air."

"I have nothing to say to you, sir. I just need to call for more water for my sister. Pray excuse me." Elizabeth tried to walk past him but was stopped by his strong arms around her waist, with her back touching his torso as he embraced her from behind.

"Lizzy, I cannot live without you. Please, please speak with me. Please forgive me." He pleaded, as his lips found their way to her neck and shoulder.

Elizabeth shuddered at his ministrations. *How could such a rake make me feel so alive? I am wanton for desiring his touch.*

"Please release me, Mr. Darcy. You cannot do this." Elizabeth swallowed down a sob. "Please." she entreated.

Hearing her cry, Darcy's heart broke. He behaved like a rake once again. All semblance of honor and respect and proper behavior of a gentleman had flown out of his head as soon as he was near her, and he had made her cry.

"I am so sorry. You do not know how sorry I am, Lizzy. I cannot control myself around you, and every insult, every misbehavior I ever committed against you, I wish I had not done so." He released her quickly.

Without turning around, Elizabeth quickly raced towards the kitchens to fetch the water herself.

Darcy was wretched. Georgiana was busy with her lessons with Mrs. Annesley, Bingley was working with his steward, and Richard had left yesterday. The Bennet sisters would be leaving tomorrow after church services, and he would return to his misery once again.

Miss Bingley had left him alone now and he felt safer being at Netherfield, but he wished he could retreat to Pemberley. He yearned to lift his Lizzy on his shoulder and carry her out of here and take her to his home. He wanted to make her his wife, to make her sister to Georgiana. He wished to give her everything he had to make her mistress of his homes.

Richard had reported to him all about Mrs. Bennet after the assembly, and although quite crass and loud when she visited Netherfield three days ago, he could see right away that she was trying to emulate Georgiana's manners. He remembered from Richard's reports that she was a daughter of a solicitor and that she had a brother in Cheapside who was a retailer of merchandise, as well as a sister married to the Meryton solicitor.

Georgiana had explained that Lizzy had a 1,000-pound dowry at her mother's passing and that Mr. Bingley would be a great catch for Jane, but that the ladies were so wonderful that they would be swooped up quickly by decent men of some standing. Georgiana had complimented Mr. Bingley's choice yesterday when Bingley had asked for courtship with Jane.

His sister had still begged him to allow Lizzy to visit Pemberley after Christmas and Darcy had heartily agreed, but if only Miss Elizabeth would consent. He knew she would never accept it now, but dearly wished she would. The past week spent with her under the same roof had been enlightening and he knew his heart was lost to his Lizzy forever.

After the Ball next week, I will take Georgiana home. Whether to London or Pemberley, I need to get out of here. I need to give Lizzy space as well as find my future. She positively hates me and I cannot do this to her. I cannot break her heart while she breaks mine.

Darcy took a deep breath and turned to his rooms to write a letter to his dear aunt of his frustrations and to work on his businesses to take his mind off of the seductress.

Chapter 9

"WHAT?! HOW?" Darcy yelled.

Georgiana grinned fully at her fuming brother. "It is true and I did do it! Lizzy was with me and she saw the whole thing. She even protected me, calling loudly for a crowd to approach us so we would have witnesses."

"I cannot believe it!" Darcy plopped down in his chair in astonishment. "You actually slapped George Wickham, who is in Meryton to obtain a lieutenantship, who tried to tempt you to elope with him once again?" He summarized the shocking news. "And Lizzy, I mean, Miss Elizabeth, was with you? Was she well?"

"Yes, William. She was so proud of me for handling myself against that rake. He tried to grab my arm after I slapped him and she walked between us to stop him; she told him that he was the worst of men for trying to assault a sixteen-year-old girl. The townsfolk began to gather around us and knowing Lizzy as a favorite, they began to boo him off and he ran like the coward he is. I am no longer afraid of him, William. Whatever rumors he might try to start, Lizzy warded it off by explaining to her Aunt Philips that he was a gambler and a seducer, trying to damage young ladies, even in public places like Meryton. She told her aunt that he might start fabricating stories about eloping with me or losing his inheritance from the Darcy family and to pay no attention to him. Aunt Philips, I mean, her Aunt Philips started telling everyone that they should be careful of George Wickham, as he is a known gambler and might run up debts with the merchants. I am so glad I told Lizzy about Wickham." She sat down most unladylike and laughed. "La! That was the most fun I had in… well, ever!"

Darcy stood and paced. "But Lizzy could have been hurt if Wickham tried something. You are certain she is well?" He was severely concerned for his beloved.

"Oh, yes. Lizzy was not frightened one bit. When I told her about Wickham, she placed the blame entirely on that lecher and told me that I was innocent. She was proud of you for coming to my rescue in Ramsgate and for treating me so kindly." She beamed.

"She was proud of me?" Darcy's heart thumped harder. "She thought I did well?"

"Yes, brother. She said you were a good brother and that she had known it for a long time."

Perhaps I still have a chance. Perhaps she will wish to know me better now. Darcy thought.

"Do you think there is any chance that you might befriend her now, William? Do you still find her so repulsive?" Georgiana asked innocently.

"What do you mean 'repulsive'? When did I tell you that I found her repulsive?" Darcy sharply retorted.

"Well, Lizzy told me that you found her loathsome and that you were not pleased with her. At least that was what she said in the beginning. You seem to frown whenever she is in the same room with you and she avoids you like the plague. I know you do not like each other but could you not tolerate her for my sake? She is my best friend. Although I like Mary and Kitty and Lydia quite much now, Lizzy is my favorite and she is so wonderful. Could you be nicer to her, William? Please, please?" She begged.

"Oh, Georgiana, I find her tolerable." *More than tolerable! I am in love with her.* "But she dislikes me and it seems we are continuing to build our misunderstandings of each other to the point that we cannot be in the same room together. I am sorry, sweetling. I truly did not mean to offend. I will try to be nicer. I *have* been trying to be nicer but she avoids me because I have made... I have been not very nice to her. Yes, I will be nicer." He did not know how much more he could share. He remembered Lizzy's tears and his heart broke again.

Georgiana, not knowing her brother's condition, cheerfully commented. "Perhaps you can ask her for the first dance at the Ball when we call on them tomorrow. You will join Mr. Bingley tomorrow when he visits to invite them to the Ball in person, will you not? It has been so nice to make calls with Mr. Bingley and chaperone with Lizzy when he takes his walks with Jane, but I do wish you would also join us. Mrs. Bennet is quite nice, I have found, and I like Mr. Bennet very much. He is similar to Lizzy and he makes me laugh." She placed a biscuit in her mouth and took a sip of her tea. "Mrs. Annesley said Kitty and Lydia are taking her lessons very well and she thanks you for allowing her to spend some time with the young Bennet girls. Mr. Bennet has been very generous and gave her a ten-pound note in gratitude."

Ten pounds. That sounds familiar. Darcy's memory flashed once again to the day of his injury. He remembered holding the disfigured Lizzy in his arms and finding her attractive even then. He thought her a servant at one time and still found her irresistible. *Even when a monster, even when I thought her a servant, I still fell in love with her.*

"I will try, sweetling. I will ask and she may deny me, or she may not because she cannot refuse a dance and still hate me, but I will call on her with you tomorrow and ask her to dance with me." He sighed. He took his seat and sipped his tea with his sister. "I will need to write to Richard about Wickham. He might not be able to take another holiday so soon after his last one but perhaps he can find some business with the militia here and get Wickham transferred somewhere else. Maybe some place cold and desolate." They laughed.

"I have a feeling Wickham will welcome it after Aunt Philips is through with him. She adores me, you know. She told me that I was responsible for helping Kitty and Lydia act like proper ladies and she said I had the best manners she had ever seen. Who would have thought Mrs. Younge's poking me with her stick at every slouch and forgetting to say 'please' and 'thank you' would reward me at the end?" They heartily laughed.

~~*~*~*~*

"Miss Elizabeth," Darcy bowed formally, even though his heart was beating as if he had been sprinting across the field.

"Mr. Darcy." Elizabeth curtseyed, avoiding his eyes. She quickly turned and spoke with Georgiana more animatedly.

Darcy closed his eyes to prepare himself to suffer for the next half hour. A sniveling man of the cloth had appeared at his side and he would not cease his speech.

"Oh, Mr. Darcy, Miss Darcy, it is such a pleasure to meet you," the man continued his speech. "I last saw Lady Catherine and her most graceful daughter, Miss de Bourgh, four days and two hours ago, and they were in most excellent health. Lady Catherine was most insistent that I should travel to my cousin's home during the early morning where the roads are better kept and of course Rosings has no bad roads, as all of them are kept most excellent and..." Mr. Collins blabbered on and on.

"Thank you, Mr. Collins, that is quite sufficient." Mr. Bennet interrupted. "Mr. Darcy, it is a pleasure to see you again. I know we have met only a couple of times, at Lucas Lodge and at the officers' dinner, and we have not had a chance to speak much," The elderly man noted the frustration in the young man's eyes as his *very* distant cousin extolled Lady Catherine's manners, property, lineage, and the cost of her chimneypiece without taking a breath. "If you are available, will you spend a little bit of time with me in my study before you return to Netherfield? I understand you have a large estate and I would like to ask you some questions."

"But of course, Mr. Bennet." Darcy smiled softly. He liked Mr. Bennet, who was intelligent and quick-witted like Lizzy. "It would be my honor."

From the corner of his eyes, he could see Elizabeth startle at his response. *Does she think of me so arrogant that I would refuse her father's request? Damn it, Lizzy! Face me and speak to me. I would do anything for you.*

"Miss Elizabeth," Darcy called out. "I see that Bingley is desiring to take a walk through the gardens. Would you mind walking out with me to chaperone them? Georgiana had wished to spend some time on the pianoforte with Miss Mary today and I had promised to do my share in chaperoning duties." He flashed a smile, hoping she would not deny him in front of an audience.

Elizabeth rolled her eyes in his full view. "Yes, Mr. Darcy. I would *love* to walk and chaperone my sister with you." She quietly huffed. "You are wicked." She whispered when standing next to him.

He leaned in and replied softly, "Wickedly handsome, Lizzy."

She could not hold in her snort. "You are certainly full of yourself, Mr. Darcy." She huffed.

They walked outside where Bingley immediately escorted Jane to the far side of the gardens.

Darcy continued his speech with Elizabeth's hand on his arm. He rubbed it tenderly, "As long as you will speak with me, I will be full of anything you wish. Have I shown you inconstancy? I only wish for you to know me better, Lizzy. I know you more than you are aware. Richard had been my spy and he gave me a full accounting of your family and your personality and your history. I know things about you that you do not even know of yourself." He teased.

"And what is that, sir? What could you possibly know about me that I do not know about myself?" Elizabeth inquired, trying to appear affronted but pleased with his easy speech. Indeed, he had fascinated her from the first meeting and seeing this easy, playful side of him had been a pleasant surprise.

"That you wish to travel and see beautiful places. That you love walking, not for exercise but to discover something new." He turned his body to face her and look into her beautiful eyes. "That you find me handsome and I was the first man to kiss you and you enjoyed it. That you think of our kiss everyday and it frightens you but it also excites you."

"How could you possibly..." Elizabeth's mouth gaped. "How did you know?" She blushed, realizing that he was correct about it all.

"Because I know you, Lizzy. My heart knows you; all those things are how I feel about you. Everything you desire and fear, I feel the same." Darcy stepped closer. "You would have never stopped to help me that day if you did not wish to make a new discovery. You found me interesting and I know you think of me constantly. You would not avoid me so much if you were not so afraid."

Elizabeth took a step back and smirked. "And who was the first man to kiss you? Did you enjoy it?" She jokingly retorted.

Darcy chuckled. "No man. Just a beautiful creature who captured my soul at first sight. Even though my brain was addled and I was hallucinating, I found that beast incomparable to every woman I ever met and could not cease thinking of her."

Not wishing to frighten her away, he kept a little distance from her, although he missed having her hand on his arm. "Lizzy, will you dance the first with me at Bingley's Ball?" He asked carefully.

"I cannot." Elizabeth replied.

"You cannot avoid me forever, Lizzy. I will ask you for every set if you deny me the first." Darcy entreated.

Elizabeth laughed. "I cannot because I am dancing the first with Mr. Collins. He heard of the Ball from Aunt Philips and asked me before I was even aware of its planning."

"What does he want with you?" Darcy angrily questioned.

Elizabeth gleamed at his obvious jealousy. "The same thing all men want." She giggled at seeing Darcy's face redden further. "To dance with a lady."

Darcy could not help but laugh at her reply. *You have no idea what all men want, my dear Lizzy.*

Elizabeth asked in return, "Why are you not dancing with Miss Bingley for the first?"

"Miss Bingley? Why on earth would I dance with her?" Darcy inquired.

"Well, because... oh. Never mind." *The secret. It is still a secret engagement because he does not remember proposing to her and he does not know she might be carrying his child.* Her heart broke at the thought. *I never had him and I never will. Stop it, Lizzy! He is my friend's brother and that is all.*

"I do not plan on dancing with anyone but you, Lizzy. I wish for the first but perhaps the second? And the supper set?"

"We cannot dance two sets! One is more than enough." Elizabeth gasped.

"No, one is not enough. Second and supper. Say yes, Lizzy. Please allow me to show everyone that I wish for your attentions. Everyone will know that I wish to gain your favor." Darcy implored.

"One, William! Just one dance." Elizabeth pleaded in return. She could not abide by Miss Bingley taunting her again with their betrothal and once Mr. Darcy remembered it all, he would have to break their friendship, if this could be called as such.

Darcy's heart beat wildly and he looked around to see Bingley quietly conversing with Miss Bennet at a distance and began to drag Elizabeth behind the infamous hedgerows where no one could see them.

"I said I would agree to one dance! Where are you taking me?" Elizabeth hissed.

As soon as they ducked behind the tall bushes, Darcy grabbed Elizabeth and began to kiss her fervently. After tongues were entwined and hands pressed each other tightly, and when breaths needed to be inhaled, he finally let her go, resting his forehead on hers.

"You called me by name, Lizzy. Like Georgiana. Like my parents. Like my wife would. Good lord, I love you so much. I want you so much, Lizzy." He began to kiss her again.

Elizabeth succumbed once again to his allurement and returned his kiss ardently. She did not know it by experience but knew enough to realize that Mr. Darcy was very aroused and it brought her joy to be the cause of it. But reality soon began to sink in; she knew he could not offer her marriage and she would not be able to accept anything less. She sighed as she rested her head against his shoulder and embraced him.

"I did not realize what I called you. I should not have." She softly whispered.

"Yes, you should. You should always call me 'William', my love." Darcy felt absolute contentment with her in his arms.

"We must return. We are not courting and we are behaving most inappropriately." Elizabeth pulled herself away from his arms.

"Two dances?" Darcy flirted.

"One, Mr. Darcy!" Elizabeth's eyes twinkled. "The supper set, William."

Darcy beamed, hearing his name from her lips again. "As you wish, my love."

He kissed her hand as they turned from the hedgerow and placed her hand on his arm. They returned near Bingley and Jane to complete their duty.

Chapter 10

"Our dance, milady." Darcy bowed and proffered his arm.

He had been irate, watching Mr. Collins step on his beloved's toes several times and preening, as if that fool had an understanding with her during the first set. Elizabeth was very popular tonight and he understood perfectly well why. She was radiant in her ivory dress with pearls in her hair.

He burned with jealousy at every dance that she shared with another man and threw furious glances at those she smiled at. Mr. Collins stood near her at every chance and even though he knew their dance was nearing, Darcy was frustrated that she would continue to be at the opposite side of the room whenever she finished a set.

Finally, the time came for the supper set and he walked towards her. She was standing next to her sister Jane and Darcy scoffed at the idea of finding the blonde pretty at one point. *She is nothing to Lizzy. Where Miss Bennet smiles, my Lizzy laughs.*

Elizabeth smiled beautifully at him and stretched out her hand to hold his arm. "Yes, Mr. Darcy. I was waiting for you. I had wondered where you were all night."

"Do not tease me, woman. You know exactly where I have been." He spoke quietly. "You have been avoiding me again but I intend to take full advantage of the supper set and to dine with you. Perhaps I can convince you to dance the last with me."

"Oh, no. I do not dance two with anyone, and in fact, my dance card is full. Did you expect me to sit out, to be slighted by gentlemen who would not give consequence to a monstrous beast?" She countered.

"Good lord, Lizzy. I apologized for my awful, untrue comments already. You know I find you irresistible." Darcy hissed. "You are the handsomest woman of my acquaintance and have an inner beauty that exceeds all others." He complimented her as they began to dance.

Once the dancing began, they had enjoyed moving gracefully together so much that they found no words to match their feelings. They stepped together and separated, returning again to face each other and found themselves in their own world throughout the set, as if all others disappeared around them and they were the only ones dancing at the Ball.

They stood with only eyes for each other as the music ended. Startled into reality as they were bumped by the dancers retreating to the supper room, Darcy gathered his precious lady on his arm and walked her to the balcony.

Taking her to a private corner, he held both of her hands and kissed them reverently.

"My dearest heart, I have loved you from the first moment I saw you. I thought I was seeing a monster before me, which I later realized was my overactive brain conjuring up a character from *The Tempest*, but once I looked into your eyes, I found my heart's desire there and I could not stop dreaming of you. Even though I do not remember it all and there is still a whole day of my life unaccounted for, I know my heart and it knows you. I love you, Elizabeth Bennet. I love you with all of my heart and I beg you to consent to be my wife. Please marry me and make me the happiest of men." Darcy awaited her answer.

Seeing the tears roll down, he continued, "I do not like to see you cry, Lizzy. I hope these are happy tears."

"Oh, William," she quietly whispered before lowering her head. After several deep breaths, she met his eyes once again and spoke softly. "I am so sorry. I cannot marry you. I dearly wish I could but I cannot." She began to wipe her face with the back of her hands until Darcy handed her his handkerchief.

"Why can you not?" Darcy gruffly asked. He felt wounded at her refusal but she had been worth every pain, every heartache, and he was determined to make her love him; to show her that he was worth a chance. "Do you love another?"

Elizabeth softly smiled. "No, I do not love another. But once you remember, once your memory returns, you will not be able to marry me and you will forget me soon enough. I am expecting a proposal from Mr. Collins soon and I have decided to accept him. He will be master of Longbourn someday and will be respectable."

"NO! Surely you are jesting. You cannot marry him! You cannot marry anyone else but me!" Darcy practically shouted. Calming a little, seeing that he was drawing the attention of the few people on the other side of the balcony, he pulled her further behind a tall planter and hid her with his body. "Marry me, Lizzy. I love you. And I know you love me!" He began to kiss her lips but stopped when he did not feel her return it.

"You will marry that *fool* and make yourself miserable? Why? If you are mercenary, why not marry me? I have enough wealth for you to fill the bathtub with jewels. Marry me. If you do not love me, marry me for my money. If you want Longbourn, I will find a way to purchase it for you.

But, if you do love me," he cradled his hands around her cheeks, "marry me to save me. I cannot envision my life without you. Even during my recovery, during my slumber, you were always there and I have always needed you. Tell me you love me. Tell me, Lizzy."

"I... I cannot..." Elizabeth cried harder. "There are things that you do not remember, William, and it is not my secret to tell. Please believe me that I cannot marry you, not because I do not wish it, but it is impossible for me to accept."

Darcy angrily released her and stepped back. "But why must you marry that, that *idiot*, then?"

"Because I believe it will help you to get over me. I can continue to be a friend to Georgiana and you will be free to move on with the path you have already begun. I release you, William, from whatever we are to each other. I must go. My family will be looking for me."

And within seconds, she was gone.

~~*~*~*~*

Darcy stood in the cold air for how long he did not know, until he heard the balcony doors open and people began to walk out after partaking their meals.

He rushed inside to find Lizzy again. He could not let her go yet. He had to see her again.

He walked from room to room and found all of the Bennets and Mr. Collins, except for Mr. Bennet and Elizabeth.

Darcy walked over to Jane. "Miss Bennet, I am looking for your sister, Miss Elizabeth. Do you know where I might find her?" He asked as calmly as possible.

"Oh, I am sorry, Mr. Darcy. She had a terrible headache and my father escorted her home. They left almost half an hour ago." Jane gently replied.

Darcy's heart tore. "Thank you." He replied and rushed towards his rooms. He tore off his cravat and coat and poured himself a large glass of port. He swallowed it in one gulp and poured another.

She refused me and left me. She thinks there is some reason that I cannot marry her and that I simply do not remember. And she is going to marry that bumbling fool? She is going to become betrothed to another man and will be lost to me forever. That fool does not deserve her. Damn it. I do not deserve her. I have insulted her and drove her away with my abominable behaviors and although she does not hate me, she does not love me enough to marry me. I cannot stay here. I must leave in the morning.

After downing his third glass, he called for his valet and told him to inform his sister that they would be departing for London at sunrise.

Not caring to remove his clothes, he told Wilkins to wake him up early to depart and promptly fell asleep, only to dream of those beautiful eyes again, but this time, they were full of tears.

Chapter 11

Georgiana whined, "Why can we not return to Netherfield, William? It has been two weeks and your businesses must be finished by now. Mr. Bingley left last week and I thought we would be returning with him." She pouted.

Darcy had been despondent, unable to find pleasure in anything, even the company of his beloved sister. "You sound like a child, like Miss Lydia used to behave, Georgiana. I cannot..." He took a deep breath, "I am needed here a little longer. I received a letter from Bingley that he proposed to Miss Bennet and he has been accepted. After he sends word of when his wedding will take place, we will plan on how quickly we can return to Pemberley."

"Oh! I received my letter from Lizzy as well!" Georgiana happily shared.

Darcy's ears perked on hearing that name.

Georgiana continued, "She is so excited about Jane's wedding, and did Mr. Bingley tell you about the other wedding?" She excitedly asked.

"I do not wish to hear about it!" Darcy abruptly commanded. He plopped onto his chair and covered his face with both hands. He had not heard about the other wedding. Bingley had only written of his own news and nothing of Lizzy's. He knew all was lost now.

Georgiana carefully approached him. "Are you well, brother? Is it your headache again?"

My heart is broken, Georgiana, Darcy cried on the inside. Quickly wiping his face, he asked his sister quietly, "Perhaps you can call for Hastings. I believe I need to see him again."

"But of course, William. I will have Mason call for him right away." She leaned and tenderly kissed her brother's head. "I will return shortly."

Darcy stared out the window for an eternity until there was a knock on the door. He turned and had not realized that Georgiana had been sitting with him the entire time without speaking. He softly smiled at his gentle sister and bid the doctor to enter.

"Hastings, thank you for coming to see me." Darcy shook the young man's hand.

"Of course, Darcy. I understand your headache has returned. Miss Darcy." Dr. Hastings bowed to the young lady and looked over Darcy with his expert eyes.

"Georgiana, I am in good hands. I will see you for dinner, sister." Darcy excused his sister to take her leave.

After the door closed, Darcy immediately began. "Hastings, I needed to talk to you about my hallucinations that I experienced before my injury. I still cannot understand what would cause me to see monsters." He pulled out the notebook that Richard had begun at Netherfield and showed him his findings. "My memory has begun to return bits and pieces and I do not understand it all, but it seems that my visions began *before* my fall. I remembered Li… a witness telling me that my horse reared up wildly and then I fell. I vaguely recall being attacked by tree branches that were swinging at me and I believe I pulled on the reins too hard to cause the fall.

"If my delusions began before I hit my head, what in the world could cause such a thing? I had thought I saw things because I hit my head but it does not appear to be the case." Darcy paced back and forth in front of the fireplace.

Hastings contemplated Darcy's story and took several notes himself.

"Do you have any recollection of anything before the accident?" Hastings asked.

"Only short bursts. I remembered what book I was reading in the carriage from my travels, a flash of Caroline Bingley trying to compromise me in my room, and Wilkins, my valet, supplied the rest of the event and assured me that she was not successful. Bingley mentioned my being angry the morning after, before I departed for my ride, after drinking coff..." Darcy stood stock-still. "He said Caroline Bingley served me a cup of coffee. Is it possible she put something in it?" Darcy questioned.

Hastings rubbed his fingers on his chin in deep thought. "Hmm, there are several herbal tonics that could cause such hallucinations. One popular one that is still used by the gypsies is henbane, which is believed to be a magic herb to make love potions. Some believe that it causes the mind to see and feel things that causes one to fall in love, but in higher doses, it could be fatal. If that harridan poured too much of it into your coffee, she could have killed you!"

"That wretched woman! First she poisons me and then lies to me that I proposed to her and slept with her! She demanded that I marry her and I believe she even stole my mother's ring. How much more damage can one woman cause?" Darcy fumed.

Hastings sneered, "She accused you of sleeping with her? How laughable! She is ridiculous. Even though she has some beauty and a large dowry, everyone who knows you, truly knows you, would never believe it. Ever since university, you built yourself a solid reputation of never dallying with anyone." He chuckled. "Remember the time we coerced you to finally visit that brothel with us?"

Darcy laughed, "You and Richard practically dragged me after pouring several drinks down my throat and told me to enjoy myself with that woman with the," he motioned his hands in front of his chest, "VERY large bosoms, and you and my cousin laughed at me when I literally ran from her room screaming." They burst out in laughter. "I saw you and Richard both standing at your doors with your trousers down to your ankles, and I think you heard me curse more than I had ever done in my life combined that day."

After the chuckles died down, Darcy continued, "I had made a promise, a vow, to my father, that I would remain chaste until my marriage, and I plan to keep it. I am not without *all* knowledge of it; I do have a little experience, even if not the actual act, but I must keep my promise to my father. I have been tempted but never by Caroline Bingley and she is the last woman... No, even if she were the last woman in the world, I would rather die than consummate with that shrew. I detest her, now more than ever."

Doctor Hastings quietly listened to his lifelong friend. They had grown up together and knew each other well. He waited for Darcy to share more of his thoughts.

"I am in love, Hastings. My head does not hurt so much as does my heart. Do you think I fell in love with her because of the love potion? This woman, this woman that I cannot marry; she cared for me after my fall and tended to my wound. I envisioned her as a hideous monster, like Caliban from *The Tempest*, and she looked horribly disfigured to me, but I fell in love with her even then. After I recovered, I met her and found her beautiful, inside and out, but now I wonder, could it have been the love potion that actually worked? Was it effective in moving my heart to feel something that would not have actually existed?" Darcy solemnly asked.

"Do you love her now? What is your first thought when you awake? When you fall asleep?" Hastings inquired gently.

Darcy closed his eyes and leaned back into his chair. "I only think of her. I dream of her, I see her beautiful eyes, and I have never felt so much for another human being before. I love my sister, I loved my parents, but this is different. She completely confuses me and infuriates me but I cannot imagine life without her and I am most miserable that she will not be with me. I would break my vows for her. If she would have me, I would give away Pemberley to be with her." Darcy growled. "But she is engaged to a complete nitwit and all I can dream of is to kidnap her and take her to Gretna Green and marry her." He rubbed his face. "I cannot take her away against her will, even if that idiot does not deserve her."

"I am sorry to hear it, Darcy. I know you have been waiting a long time to find a wife." Hastings consoled. "You are truly in love with her. A love potion would not last so long, if such a thing existed, and what you feel, the love you have for her, is not a fleeting one. I have not found such a love but it sounds fierce and strong. I do not envy you the pain but wish you happiness. I hope you will find another to love or to find a way to marry this woman."

"I will never love another. I will never marry anyone but her." Darcy declared. "I do not know how I will handle Caroline Bingley; she has been a thorn in my side ever since meeting Bingley. How she believes herself to be so above others and thinks herself worthy to be mistress of Pemberley is incomprehensible, but I have only tolerated her for Bingley's sake. Well, no more. I will not invite her to Pemberley or reside under the same roof ever again. I need to find a way to prove that she either reproduced my mother's ring or has stolen it somehow. I had meant to write to Mrs. Reynolds but I keep forgetting."

"You did have quite a lot on your mind lately, Darcy." Hastings chuckled. "Just let me know how I can assist you." He looked at his pocket watch. "I must go visit another patient of mine. His gout has been causing problems and he is very unhappy with me that I will not let him travel to Bath yet." He stood. "Do you wish for some tonics? Shall I send a note to the apothecary?"

Darcy stood as well. "No, no. I have no pains that any medicine will cure. Thank you, Hastings. I am glad to have your ear. I have been keeping too much to myself. I will have to face her once more for Bingley's wedding then I will retreat to Pemberley. I plan on hiding myself there for a while so I do not know when I will see you again." He chuckled to himself, "Perhaps I can find this love potion and make her fall madly in love with me."

He shook his friend's hand and watched him depart. Darcy sat at his desk to compose several letters, including one to his favorite aunt and another to his housekeeper to investigate the status of his mother's ring.

Chapter 12

"Miss Eliza! You look quite sickly. Are you ill?" Caroline covered her nose and mouth with her handkerchief, in case this woman might be infectious.

Elizabeth hid her smirk. *She will never change, will she?* "I am well, Miss Bingley. Just a little melancholy. My dear Jane is going to marry your brother next week and I am saddened to lose her company, even if she will only be three miles away." She replied.

Caroline straightened her posture and tucked her handkerchief away. "Well, it is a great privilege to be mistress here and I hope your sister will know what to do. I will be sure to guide her in *many* ways to be a proper mistress of such a grand estate."

"My sister knows very well of her duties, as one who has grown up on an estate *all* her life, Miss Bingley. I am certain you will be free to spend your time with your... other entertainments... once my sister takes her place as mistress here." Elizabeth countered.

Caroline sneered, "But of course. I will be marrying myself and I will be busy planning a grand wedding as well as learning all of the duties of being Mistress of Pemberley. Mr. Darcy will be returning for the wedding tomorrow and I am certain we will set a date soon." She looked down her nose at the country bumpkin. "Pemberley is the greatest estate in the whole of England and I will become Mrs. Darcy and take *my* rightful place."

Elizabeth paled at her statement but quickly recovered. "Congratulations. His memory has returned?" She took a calming breath. "And your babe, are you both doing well?"

Caroline cursed under her breath. She had completely forgotten that she told Miss Eliza that she was already carrying Darcy's heir.

It was now January and Jane and Charles would marry in a week. If she had truly become impregnated in early October, she would be three months along and would begin to show signs of carrying soon. It was too bad that she could not get someone else to put her in that state.

"Well, I... I am... I lost the babe. I am certain I will be with child again soon as soon as..." her head sparked another thought, "as soon as Fitzwilliam returns and takes me to his bed. He was insatiable during our night together and I know he will want me as soon as he sees me again. It has been more than a month since we last saw each other and he will desire to be with me the moment he sees me." She jeered, seeing Miss Eliza's pretty face pale again. "Whatever his attentions may have been to you, Miss Eliza, he loves me and I WILL marry him."

"Congratulations. Pray, excuse me." Elizabeth quickly departed to return to her sister's side, who was speaking with Mrs. Nicholls on making changes to the mistress' rooms.

How will I face him again? I have thought of him constantly but I dread seeing him again. Elizabeth thought.

~~*~*~*~*

"Lizzy! Where have you been?" Her mother shrieked. "Lieutenant Denny came by to call and he has been sharing all kinds of news with us! Such a handsome officer. He told us all about Mr. Wickham! That villainous man that Miss Darcy warned us about apparently left TWO servant maids *with child*," she whispered the last part, "and ran up enough gambling debts with the other officers to be flogged!" She waved her handkerchief in the air as she fluttered about, "Can you imagine such a thing? Such a dissolute man to be an officer!"

Kitty chimed in, "I am so glad Georgiana warned us of his character. Even though he is very handsome, he is not a good man and we might have been deceived by him."

Lydia added her piece, "Well, I would have never been tricked by a man like that. I am certain I would have resisted him and seen through his lies right away. Poor Mary King. She will be ridiculed for being courted by such a disreputable man. It is terrible she did not know what he was and agreed to courtship when she returned a week ago. I hope she is not with child herself and quits the courtship quickly! I knew he never cared three straws about her. Who could, about such a nasty little freckled thing?"

"Do not be unkind, Lydia Bennet. Mary King is a very nice young lady who is shy and was taken advantage of. Her inheritance of 10,000 pounds brought her the attentions of that unworthy man but perhaps she will find happiness with one who will love her for herself someday." Elizabeth chastised. She thought of Georgiana and her friend's heartbreak over the summer, which naturally led to her older brother.

Elizabeth quickly shook off her reverie as Jane commented, "Perhaps Mr. Wickham is not as bad as reported. There must be some goodness in him."

Elizabeth smiled, "Oh, Jane, I know you would have willingly gone through the world without believing that so much wickedness existed in the whole race of mankind, but it is indeed true, that much evil is collected in one individual here and Mr. Wickham is fully to blame, I am certain of it."

"Well, I always knew he was evil! As soon as my sister Philips told me about his character and his lies, I knew he was up to no good. I am glad we never invited him here at Longbourn. It would have been disgraceful to have shared a meal with him!" Mrs. Bennet expressed her opinions. "Now, girls, we must make sure our dresses are ready. Lizzy! Your walk was too long. Run along. Get your pretty new dress out for the wedding. It needs more lace!"

Elizabeth rolled her eyes as she stood to fetch it. "Yes, mama." She walked to her room where she sat on her bed to look out the window. *I wonder if I will see him soon.* She felt her eyes fill with tears once again. *I must overcome this. I must. All is lost to me but he will find happiness.*

She returned to her task and joined her mother and sisters downstairs to work on their dresses.

~~*~*~*~*

"No, Georgiana. It is past calling hours and you should wait until tomorrow." Darcy beckoned.

"But it has never stopped us before. I dearly wish to go see Lizzy. Oh, please, William!" Georgiana begged.

Darcy gave her a stern look. "Bingley has told me that Miss Bennet had already visited this morning and he does not intend to call at Longbourn today. We will have dinner in two hours and you can see her tomorrow." He ran his fingers through his hair. "I am tired, sweetling. I would like to rest for a while."

"I understand, William. I only wish we had left town earlier so we could have made our call today, but I will be patient. Lizzy's letters have been worrisome and I am anxious to see her but as long as I can spend some time with her soon, I am willing to wait." Georgiana told her brother.

"What is worrisome? Is she not happy with the wedding?" Darcy asked abruptly. He was concerned that Elizabeth might be unhappy. *I would carry her off to Scotland right now if she asked it of me. If she would only consent to be with me, I would give up everything.*

Georgiana replied, "Of course she is happy with the weddings. It has been exciting to have two weddings a week apart in this little town. I believe she is just a little sad about having Jane live afar, even if it is only three miles away. I am certain all will be well."

Darcy burned in jealousy once again. *She is happy. Damn it. It is truly all lost.* "If you will excuse me, Georgiana, I will rest."

"But of course, brother. See you for dinner." Georgiana quickly left his sitting room to rest as well.

Darcy locked the door behind her and placed a chair against it. He had only agreed to reside at Netherfield once more as a concession to Bingley after his friend promised to place extra footmen near his rooms and to take all of the keys away from Caroline. He promised that Darcy would be kept safe for the four nights before the wedding.

Richard had joined their party as well, as his cousin was able to request an assignment to oversee the militia located here. Richard had wanted to see Wickham for himself and to arrange for a transfer to Newcastle this winter. He had already exchanged communications with Colonel Forster, who was leading this group, and after receiving some news of gambling debts, it was agreed upon to complete the transfer this week.

Darcy sat on the very chair he moved to block the door. *Tomorrow. I will see her tomorrow. I dread seeing her but I am most impatient at the same time. I can only hope she will be civil.*

Chapter 13

"*What in damnation?!*" He remembered yelling. Darcy sat on Perseus, his stallion, and looked at the tree, recognizing it as the one that had attacked him before.

He dismounted his horse and walked over to the tree, touching it cautiously, as if it might come back alive. He let out a breath after knocking on the trunk and finding it solid and immovable.

Darcy looked around the area and found it a normal vista, just like any other hillside, and yet he felt connected to this place more than his own home. His heart had been here, where he had met Lizzy, and everything had changed. His life had turned upside down that day of his injury and although Miss Bingley might have been to blame for it, he could not regret meeting and falling in love with his Lizzy.

His attention snapped to the present when he heard a twig break. He looked up and saw the woman of his dreams fifty yards away, frozen in her track as she saw him and his horse.

Their eyes met, for what seemed to be several long minutes, then they rushed to embrace each other, Darcy lifting her up into his arms, and they began to kiss ardently, until their arms were wrapped around the other and no forces could tear their souls apart.

Eventually, as they parted for breath, Elizabeth spoke first. "I do not know what power you have over me but I have missed you. I do not know how I will live without you but for now, right now, I wish to stay in your arms."

"You never have to leave me. Just say the word and I will take you to Scotland right now. Let us elope and marry. Be mine, Lizzy. Let us get on Perseus and ride off and never look back." Darcy implored.

Elizabeth laughed while holding his body against hers and resting her head on his chest. "If only it were so simple, William, I would run away with you right now. But alas, we have our duties and we cannot be so dishonorable." She squeezed him tighter with her arms. "I did not think I would see you so early this morning. I had thought you and Georgiana would call on me at Longbourn later today."

"My sister is most determined to see you. She has missed you so much, but not as much as I have. My love, you belong with me. You belong in my arms." He led her to the foot of the tree. "Will you sit with me a little? Stay with me a little longer?" He feared she would run off again.

"Yes, William. Just for a little while longer." Elizabeth sat on the ground.

Darcy held her in his arms as he leaned against the tree trunk. They looked out to the landscape and sat quietly, contemplating how much time they had left together.

"When is the wedding, Lizzy?" Darcy finally asked. *I will spend every moment with her like this before she is out of my reach.*

"In three days. You know this. Will you not be standing up with Mr. Bingley?" Elizabeth asked in confusion. She looked up to see his face to assess if he might be having another illusion.

"Not Bingley's, yours, Lizzy!" Darcy complained. "When is *your* wedding?"

"And who am I marrying, William? I do not understand." Elizabeth sat up straight.

Darcy growled. "You are marrying Mr. Collins, that bumbling fool who will get Longbourn. That jackass who does not deserve you."

Elizabeth laughed. "I am not! I wrote to Georgiana that I could not accept him even after he asked three tim..." Elizabeth could not continue her speech, as Darcy's lips landed on hers and he kissed her most passionately, placing her head on the ground and laying over her.

Darcy cradled her head and made love to her mouth with his, one hand stroking her hair while the other began to caress her shoulder and leading down to her breast. He brushed his hand over her chest, her delicate waist, then squeezed her hip, positioning himself over her to coax her legs to open as he lay over her to connect with her as closely as possible over their clothing.

"I love you. You are not marrying that idiot. Marry me. Be my wife. I thought you were to be his and I despaired. There is no impediment now. Marry me, Lizzy." He continued his kisses on her neck and shoulder and sank lower to land on her décolletage.

Elizabeth was enraptured by the sensation of his hands and lips on her body. As she felt his lips on her breast, she suddenly realized that he had exposed her chest completely and his tongue was on her areola. She gasped at such an intimate pleasure but when his hand travelled down to lift her dress up, she snapped to attention that she was going to be compromised beyond what she should give.

"Stop. William, I said stop!" She yelled as she pushed him off of her.

Darcy had been in the throes of passion and had not realized that he was ready to take her virtue. He released her immediately and began to apologize.

"I am so sorry, Lizzy. I... I had not comprehended that I was about to... I love you so much and I want all of you. I wish to make you my wife. I would make you my wife right now if you would have me, Lizzy." He pleaded. "You must marry me. I cannot be without you."

Elizabeth stood angrily. "Is this how you propose to all women? You promise them wealth and comfort and take their virtues, only to forget your commitment and chase another woman? I cannot believe I almost succumbed to your seductions. I almost... Well, I did not and I will not! You must keep away from me, Mr. Darcy. I will not fall for it. No matter how handsome you are, I will not lose myself in my passions." She straightened her clothing and began to fix her hair.

She continued speaking, "Even if you do not remember everything, you must know that Miss Bingley will not release you. I do not think you love her, even if she believes it, but she carried your child and you are engaged to her! I may not be betrothed, but you, sir, are!"

"I AM NOT ENGAGED TO HER!" Darcy yelled. "I have *never* been engaged to her."

Elizabeth scoffed, "You just do not remember yet. She showed me your mother's ring. She told me that you begged her to marry her and ravished her for hours. Just like you were attempting to do with me. She carried your child but lost it and she told me you would take her again as soon as you returned. Did you lay with her last night? Did you impregnate her again?" Elizabeth fumed at the thought of Darcy with that woman. She growled, "I hate you, William. Do not come near me again!"

Darcy was indignant and grabbed her arm to stop her from walking away. She turned and attempted to slap him again but he was quick this time and stopped her hand from reaching his face. "Do not, Lizzy. I am innocent."

"I do not believe you." She spat. After she shook her wrist from his grip, she gave him a look of disgust. "Send Georgiana to call at Longbourn but do not come. If you do, I will not acknowledge you. I wash my hands of you, Mr. Darcy. You are a seducer and I only blame myself for falling into your trap. You would have abandoned me with a child high in my belly and I would have been ruined forever. My sisters would have been ruined by association and you still would have left me for the wealthy woman with her 20,000 pounds who would be a *proper* mistress of Pemberley."

"I am innocent! Please listen to..." Darcy could not make her hear him.

Elizabeth wiped her tears. "I am tired, William. We cannot go on like this. I released you before, I release you again. Please let me go and do not return." She stormed off while Darcy stood frozen.

Darcy watched her run down the hill and disappear into the groves. He knew she was not willing to listen. He, who was innocent of her charges, could do naught but let her go and give her time to calm.

He was furious as he kicked the innocent tree as if to blame it for his suffering. "Aargh!" he screamed. "This is all Caroline Bingley's fault!" He jumped onto Perseus and rode the opposite direction of Lizzy. He saw a pathway that he had not been before, towards what he believed was Mr. King's estate, and rode his horse hard to work out his frustrations.

Chapter 14

After a half-hour of rough riding, Darcy slowed down his stallion and took several breaths.

It is not anyone else's fault than my own. I rushed her and took advantage of her generosity. I touched her as only her husband should and she is furious with me because I was so ungentlemanly. What have I done? How do I make her understand that I am not engaged and never have been?

Suddenly, he heard the cry of a woman and he comprehended quickly that she was being hurt. He trotted closer to where the noise was coming from and heard the voice cry out, "No! Release me! You cannot do this!"

Then he heard a familiar voice shout out, "I will take you. I will take your virtue and marry you, Mary. I want your 10,000 pounds and you cannot stop me."

"WICKHAM!" Darcy shouted. He saw his childhood friend's head pop up from behind the bushes and the young lady pushed him off quickly to run towards Darcy.

Darcy recognized the young woman as Mary King, whom he had met once when calling on her uncle. Her hair was mussed but her clothing still intact. It had been cold and it was obvious that Wickham had not yet managed to get through her many layers of dress.

Darcy jumped off his horse and handed it to the young woman. "Can you ride? Can you call for help?" He spoke gently and quietly to her.

She nodded as she wiped her tears.

After helping her onto his horse to ride astride, he patted Perseus' rear to send her off to safety.

"Wickham, I am in a great mood for some sparring today. I wish I had my foil but my fists will do." He drew nearer Wickham who was buttoning up his falls and fixing his coat jacket.

"Well, I always could beat you, Darcy. I will be more than happy to blacken your eyes and knock some of your teeth out. You stopped me from getting my hands on Georgiana's dowry and now Mary's. I never did get to sample that sister of yours, but I was so close to taking Mary. I heard you danced with that chit, one of the Bennet sisters. The one that berated me in Meryton in front of an audience. It is all her fault that I was not able to set up any credit in this hellhole town. I have been watching her at times and she is a delicious little thing. I heard she is penniless but I should have paid her a little more attention. I am sure she would have opened her legs to enjoy my attentions and I would have taken her again and again to ruin her, if only to make you miserable, you bastard." He jumped at Darcy to throw the first punch.

Darcy quickly dodged his jab and landed a blow to Wickham's shoulder. Wickham might have been able to beat him before but it was when they were children, and Darcy had been very active with his pugilist and fencing lessons for the past decade.

Darcy stepped around him and punched Wickham's side hard, hearing a crack on his former friend's ribs. "That is for Georgiana." He grabbed the lieutenant's arm with one hand and landed another hit onto that man's stomach. "That is for every woman you injured in the past years," and he finally closed his fist tighter and lobbed his final strike on his jaw. "That is for Lizzy."

Wickham landed flat on his back, completely unconscious and definitively beaten.

"No one threatens my Lizzy. She is going to be my wife, you ass!" He spat on Wickham.

Darcy puffed out several breaths and stood tall. It had felt good to get some exercise after the miserable morning he had been having.

In a few minutes, he saw two riders approach with his own horse unseated.

He was surprised that Richard was arriving with Mr. King but relieved that his cousin would be able to take Wickham into custody to Colonel Forster.

"Richard, what are you doing here?" Darcy asked.

Richard dismounted quickly. "I was taking a report for Wickham's misconducts early this morning and was calling on Mr. King, when Miss King arrived on your horse and told us what happened." He looked at where Wickham was laying with his limbs spread out. "You took care of him already, did you now?" He laughed.

Darcy laughed as well, as he walked around and patted Perseus. "It was good to get some exercise. He thought he could beat me but he did not get near me once." He gloated.

"Thank you for coming to my niece's rescue, Mr. Darcy. I do not know what would have happened if you did not arrive in time." Mr. King gratefully shook his hand. "If there is anything I can do, anything at all, do not hesitate."

"Mr. King is also the magistrate in town. It is too bad we cannot expose Wickham for his villainy today. He could have done anything he wanted with her and suffer no consequences, but if rumor gets out that Miss King might have been compromised, she will be ruined. These rules are so archaic; it is most unfair to innocent women." Richard criticized. He had found Miss King quite pleasant and her freckles were adorable.

Darcy commented, "Well, perhaps we can report this as conduct unbecoming an officer and have him transferred immediately. TODAY, Richard." He grew angry once again, remembering Wickham's words about Lizzy and the thought of his ruining countless women in his past.

Just then, Darcy saw movement from the corner of his eyes of Wickham running with a saber pointing at him. In a flash, he turned and saw Richard rush him from the side, throwing his body on top of Wickham's to the ground. Wickham lost his grip on his sword and Richard loomed over him, landing blow after blow, as he sat on his torso.

Richard ceased his strikes when he looked down to see Wickham unconscious, with his mouth, nose, and eyes covered in blood. Richard took a deep breath and stood over him. He pulled out his own saber and in a calm precision, sliced an 'X' on the scoundrel's forehead that would leave a scar to mark him like a criminal, but not deep enough to cause death.

Richard sighed, "He will never bother anyone again. Anyone who sees him will see a scoundrel and no one will ever think him handsome again." He checked Wickham's body for more weapons and finding none, commanded to Mr. King and Darcy, "Help me pull him up onto my horse. He will need medical care before he is transferred out of Meryton. If only I could get him to the continent and put him in front of Bony himself!"

Darcy joined Richard and Mr. King to ride to the encampment where he sent a quick note to inform Georgiana what had happened and that it would take several hours to settle the situation with Colonel Forster.

~~*~*~*~*

"I am so pleased to see you, Georgiana! I have missed you dearly, my friend." Elizabeth embraced Miss Darcy. She was relieved that Mr. Darcy had acceded to her request to not make the visit and was able to relax with her young friend.

Georgiana excitedly greeted the other ladies. Mr. Bingley had escorted her and Mrs. Annesley to Longbourn and Mrs. Annesley was very pleased to see the young ladies curtsey and greet everyone properly.

While Kitty and Lydia gracefully informed Mrs. Annesley of the latest news with their mother, Mary sat near Jane and Mr. Bingley to chaperone them for the last few days before their wedding and Georgiana quietly spoke with her favorite.

"How have you been, Lizzy? Your letters seemed morose in comparison to our conversations before the Ball but I thought you would be happy to be rid of Mr. Collins' attentions. Are you wishing you had agreed to marry him?" Georgiana started.

Elizabeth chuckled. "Not a chance, Georgiana!" The younger lady merrily giggled. "I am so glad my friend Charlotte is marrying that odious man. No matter how many compliments he gave me, he professed to fall madly in love with Charlotte and became engaged to her three days after he proposed to me." She smiled softly, "You know I will marry only for the deepest love. Just like you promised me, Georgiana." She held her friend's hand and squeezed it. "And your brother, is he fully recovered?" She asked carefully.

"He has been sullen for some reason but I believe he is well now. He still has headaches at times but he has no other complaints. He says his memory comes in pieces but he will most likely never recover the whole period. He has been beyond grumpy in town but he seems to be happy to be back." Georgiana replied.

Elizabeth sighed, "It must be due to returning to Miss Bingley's side. Do you know if a date has been set?"

"A date for what?" Georgiana asked. "He hates Miss Bingley; why should he be happy to see her?"

Elizabeth gasped quietly. "Oh, I have forgotten again. Miss Bingley has asked me to not mention it until Mr. Darcy's memories return, but they...

they are engaged, Georgiana. Surely she must have shared it with you. She has been more than happy to mention it every time I visit her."

"William is not engaged. What makes you think that? Miss Bingley is lying to you. How long has she been telling you of this?" Georgiana hissed loudly, drawing the attention of the others in the room.

Elizabeth spoke at a louder volume. "But of course, Georgiana. I know you wish to go outside. Mama, Mr. Bingley, if you will excuse us, my dear friend and I have many things to catch up on."

Finally, after putting their coats on and stepping outside where they could have some privacy, Elizabeth continued, "Miss Bingley has kept it a secret and I am sorry to be the one to break her confidence, Georgiana. Your brother proposed to her after Michaelmas and after he suffered his injury, he could not remember it but he had given her your mother's ring as a promise. They... They have become one flesh and he will have to marry her. Even if his memory does not return, he cannot abandon his honor, Georgiana."

"That is ridiculous! He would never! You say that he is an honorable man but what honorable man would take a lady's virtue before marriage?" Georgiana questioned.

"Georgiana," Elizabeth attempted to placate her friend while not knowing how much to share about a man's intentions, "I know you think your brother the best of men..."

"No, Lizzy. He would never. He is a man, I know, but he made a vow. He made a vow to Father and he would never break it." Georgiana adamantly stated.

But he almost... well, perhaps not so far but he and I... Elizabeth's thoughts were interrupted when a large landau entered the estate and stopped at the front door.

Georgiana gasped loudly, "Oh, no! What is she doing here?!" Georgiana ran towards the carriage and saw Lady Catherine step out.

"Aunt Catherine, what are you doing here? What has happened? Is Anne well?" Georgiana rushed to her side and embraced her.

Lady Catherine patted her niece's back. "Hello, child. What are *you* doing here? We are all well. Anne remains at Rosings with Mrs. Jenkinson. I have come to speak with a Miss Elizabeth Bennet. Do you know her?"

Georgiana breathed a sigh of relief. "This is she." She waited until Miss Elizabeth neared the carriage. "Miss Elizabeth Bennet, my aunt, Lady Catherine de Bourgh of Rosings." Georgiana made the introductions.

"Georgie, please return to the house and inform the..." Lady Catherine looked at the exterior of the modest home, "inhabitants of this place of who I am. I desire a moment of Miss Bennet's time and walk," she looked at the garden where her niece had just exited, "in that prettyish kind of a little wilderness there."

"But of course, aunt." Georgiana replied. "I will go in now, Lizzy."

Elizabeth could only nod and await what this grand lady might have to say to her.

"Miss Bennet," her ladyship began, in an angry tone, "you ought to know that I am not to be trifled with. A report of a most alarming nature reached me two months ago and I had dismissed it as youthful frivolity, but then another letter was sent to me last month. I had been concerned but after hearing more from Mr. Collins directly yesterday and understanding your sister is to be married to Mr. Bingley, I instantly resolved on setting off for this place, that I might make my sentiments known to you."

"And what would you like to make known to me, madam?" Elizabeth inquired.

"You do not deserve him. He is too good for you. Darcy is the most honorable and dutiful man in all of England and I am the closest family he has. He wrote to me of his heartbreak that you had refused him, most stubbornly at that, after he had begged you to marry him at Netherfield Ball. You used him most ill and denied him and I had hoped that all would be resolved soon, but when he wrote to me last month and told me that you were marrying another, I advised him to seek a better woman and to not spend one more minute on such a worthless woman.

"I was able to put one and one together after Mr. Collins explained after his interminable disclosures of everything that was going on here in Hertfordshire, and finally realized that Darcy believed you to be marrying Mr. Collins and I know that Mr. Collins is marrying a Miss Charlotte Lucas. There seems to be some confusion around who is marrying who, and you, young lady, are in the thick of it all! I do not understand how any intelligent woman could refuse my nephew.

"If only my Anne was healthy enough to marry, I would have pressed him to marry my daughter. They would have been perfect for each other; from the same noble line, with a splendid fortune on both sides. But I know that Anne would only suffer should she attempt to bear an heir, and Darcy needs a strong, intelligent wife to be able to help him manage his estate as well as bring some comfort in his lonely life. He and Georgiana have suffered too long with mercenary men and women who only seek their own gain, and I truly wish for my dearest sister's children to find happiness.

"You do not deserve him. Why do you keep pulling on the string around his heart to make him so miserable, Miss Bennet? By what right do you make him suffer so? Is it to increase his affections? Is it to bring him misery; to force him to fall on his knees and to beg for mercy? Do you love him at least a little?" She demanded.

"OF COURSE, I LOVE HIM!" Elizabeth shouted. "I have never loved deeper nor greater and I only wish for his happiness. I am most acutely grieved. I cannot eat, I cannot sleep, and I cry every time I think of him." Her tears began to roll down.

Elizabeth pulled out Darcy's handkerchief and stared at it before wiping her face. "I have loved him since the first day I met him. When I saw him bloodied and dazed, when he called me 'loathsome' and 'hideous', I still loved him then. I wish for nothing else than to be his wife but I cannot accept him. He is already engaged and she might be carrying his heir again. He does not remember proposing to this woman but he must do the honorable thing and marry her. His family name is so important to him and he simply does not remember."

Lady Catherine huffed, "And who is this woman that he supposedly impregnated? What do you mean 'his heir again'?"

Elizabeth wiped her face, "Miss Caroline Bingley. She has told me many times that they have an understanding and that he proposed to her before his accident. She has Mr. Darcy's mother's ring and although she lost the first baby, she is confident that..."

"Stop. Stop right there. First of all, Darcy has told me that he found you witty and intelligent but I think you must be rather stupid. Why in God's name would you believe anything that comes out of that deceiver's mouth? She has been a mercenary harridan from the first time she heard of Darcy's name and has done nothing but to promote herself to be his wife. She is a lecher of the worst kind and I know for a fact that Darcy would never attach himself to that... that... hag, who would do anything for wealth and connections. She cares not one bit for Darcy himself; she only wants Pemberley and all of Darcy's wealth.

"And anyone who knows him knows that he has made several vows at his father's deathbed. The elder Darcy was... well, he was a bit of a prude. He liked to follow the Good Book as well as rules of society and believed in being honest and honorable. He made Darcy swear to take care of his sister, his estate Pemberley, and to remain chaste for his future wife. There is no way in God's holy name that Darcy would break his vow for that awful woman. If he were to ever break his vows, I could see him breaking them for you, but never for Caroline Bingley.

"He told me that he had never loved anyone before and you broke his heart. All because of that conniving wench who stole my sister's ring and took advantage of Darcy's memory loss. You are a fool, Miss Bennet. You should beg him to take you if you truly love him." Lady Catherine concluded.

Elizabeth could only laugh loudly at the ridiculousness of this situation. It dawned upon her now that she only had Miss Bingley's word of the secret engagement; Darcy had not looked at that woman twice and he had never, not once, showed inconstancy in his love for herself. He had kissed her, declared his love for her, and she had been the only partner he danced with at the Ball. He favored no one else, and at every meeting, with every look and every touch, he spoke of his love for her.

"We are all fools in love, madam. And I will live with this regret for the rest of my life. I have pushed him too far. This very morning, I told him I hated him and that I did not believe him. I accused him of being a seducer and to let me go and never return. His good opinion, once lost, is lost forever." She sat on the bench and began to weep.

Lady Catherine took a seat next to her and gathered her with one arm. "There, there. It will be well. You and Darcy have much to speak of, but it will turn out all as it should. If you love him, if you make him happy, I wish for both of you to find your contentment together. Perhaps you will prove me wrong and show me that you do have some good sense and accept him when he proposes again."

Elizabeth was sobbing on her ladyship's shoulder by now. "But he will not ask again. How could he? I have abused him most cruelly." She wailed.

"If he were a lesser man, if he were not so in love, perchance he might not be able to overcome his pride to ask again, but he will. I know he will." She patted Elizabeth's shoulder.

"Thank you, milady." Elizabeth slowly sat up after her tears were spent.

"Call me Aunt Catherine, child. I believe you will be my niece soon. Very soon." She comforted Elizabeth. "Let us return. Your family must be expecting the worst, we have been gone so long. Introduce me to your family, as they will become my family soon."

They began to walk arm in arm. "And let me tell you about Mr. Collins. I have never met a stupider man but he loves to talk so much and extols so many of my virtues, I found him quite entertaining and hired him on. I do hope his new wife will be sensible. That man is harmless but needs a steady hand to make sure he does not become a complete sycophant!" Lady Catherine gleefully shared with Elizabeth, as they entered Longbourn.

Chapter 15

"Aunt Catherine! What are you doing here?" Darcy exclaimed as he entered the sitting room at Netherfield.

He had left Richard and Mr. King with Colonel Forster and returned tired but anxious to see his sister. He saw his aunt sitting with Georgiana and Bingley, taking tea and conversing pleasantly. Miss Bingley and Mrs. Hurst were nowhere to be seen, while Mr. Hurst, appearing quite sober, sat with Bingley, although quiet. He walked over and kissed Lady Catherine's cheek and sat next to her.

"I have come to fix your lovelife, Darcy. Apparently you have made quite a mess of it. Now, what is this about your being engaged to Caroline Bingley? I shooed that woman off with her sister from sitting with me but how could you get tangled up with her, of all people?" Lady Catherine inquired.

"I am NOT engaged to Caroline Bingley!" Darcy fumed, as he stood and paced. "I have never been and I will never be engaged to her. Why does everyone think that I am engaged to her?" Darcy gruffly replied.

He saw Bingley and Hurst chuckle, as he flailed his arms as if throwing a tantrum.

"Tell me about this ring of hers. Is it truly my sister's?" Her ladyship asked.

"What ring? Which one?" Georgiana innocently asked.

Darcy rubbed his face and began his story after sitting down again. "The sapphire with pearls around it, Georgiana. Miss Bingley conveniently told me that I proposed to her right before my injury, AFTER she validated that I suffered a memory loss, and showed me that ring as proof. I have been able to gather that she attempted a compromise the night before my accident and Wilkins was witness to it." He heard Georgiana gasp. "Nothing happened! She was promptly kicked out of my room but I spoke with Hastings and he believes she might have put in a potion, some ridiculous love potion that might have caused me to hallucinate and fall off my horse that next morning. If it is true, she is not only responsible for my injury and may have stolen our mother's ring, but is now telling others that she is pregnant with my child. It has been three months. You would think she would have signs of this phantom pregnancy but it has been lies. All lies." Darcy took a sip of tea that Georgiana offered and continued.

"I already approached her to cease this nonsense of an engagement but I cannot prove what has happened with the ring. I wrote to Mrs. Reynolds about it and she did report it missing from Pemberley's safe. It had not been noticed before since we all thought it locked in the safe, but I do not understand when she could have had the chance to steal it. I cannot accuse her without proof." Darcy concluded grimly.

"Oh, William," Georgiana sighed. "Have you been suffering all this time because of that ring?" She stood, "Oh dear brother, why did you not tell me earlier? Give me a few moments. I will return."

In a few minutes, Georgiana returned with her hands behind her back. She stood in front of her brother and Lady Catherine who was sitting next to him and flashed her hand. "Is this the ring that you are speaking of?"

"Yes, well, it is not identical to the one Miss Bingley was wearing, now that I look at it, but this is what I remember Mother wearing. This is the one in the portraits but Miss Bingley's might have been smaller, from what I recall. Wherever did you find it?" Darcy asked curiously.

Georgiana grinned broadly. "I never found it; I never lost it. This was Mother's favorite ring, from what Aunt Catherine told me, and I had held on to it for months. It was always safe in my jewelry box, where it has never left it. I would never lose such a precious memory of our mother."

Lady Catherine beamed. "Your father had acquired it for William's fifth birthday in thanks for her giving him an heir. I helped him fetch a good price for it, since I had to fight off some of the harpies who had wanted it. It once belonged to Queen Elizabeth, you know." She turned Georgiana's hand from side to side. "Look at the sparkle. You do not find many sapphires of this size and shine without paying a fortune for it. Your father did not care how much it cost. Anne loved blue and she wore this until the day she went to heaven. Such a beautiful ring."

"But what is the one that Miss Bingley is wearing then?" Darcy returned to the problem at hand. "It looked so similar, I thought it the same."

"You know nothing, William. When it comes to fashion and jewels, you are as clueless as... as Mr. Bingley here. No offense, Mr. Bingley." Georgiana nodded with a huge grin.

Bingley smiled cheerfully. "None taken! Go on. Tell us about the other ring."

"Well, when I was in Ramsgate last June, I found that ring at a small shop by the sea and it looked so similar to this one," she pointed to the ring on her hand, "that I decided to purchase it to wear it just for fun. I thought of giving it to Mrs. Younge but she was so mean to me that I just held on to it. I took it to Pemberley and I remember Miss Bingley asking me about the ring in the portrait and she must have thought the imitation was the original. She must have stolen it right off my dressing table, since I did not bother to lock it away. I had completely forgotten about it. I wish you had asked me sooner, William. I am no longer a child." Georgiana pouted.

Darcy stood and embraced her. "I am sorry, sweetling. I know you are a wise young lady and I am sorry I kept secrets from you. I would have never guessed.... The time that I spent in misery..." Darcy took his seat again. "It matters naught. It is over and I am free." He whispered, "If only she will have me."

Lady Catherine patted his hand. "Have hope, nephew. She loves you. She told me herself that she loves you. Go to her. Find her and make each other happy."

"Who, William?" Georgiana quietly asked with hope rising in her heart. "Could it be Lizzy? Could you possibly be in love with her?"

Darcy could only nod his head as Georgiana squealed and jumped into his arms in joy.

Bingley suddenly stood appearing very pale. "Miss Darcy…" He paced almost in circles.

"Yes, Mr. Bingley?" Georgiana could not understand why his face was blanched and what could possibly be wrong.

Bingley stopped his movement and looked at Darcy and then Miss Darcy. "If I may ask, how much did you pay for that ring?"

Darcy groaned and leaned his back, understanding his friend's question.

Georgiana innocently replied, "A guinea, actually. I thought it looked so pretty and I paid more for it than my usual trinkets. Why do you ask?"

Bingley sat down on the nearest chair. "More than a shilling. It is a capital offense." He sighed. "Darcy, I know you detest her but she is… she is still my sister..."

"We will not have her hanged, Charles. I do not wish anyone to hang and although she has caused so much misery, it has brought many discoveries that I would not trade for the world." *I might not have fallen in love with Lizzy and she might have found me an arrogant sod, caring only for status and connections. If she understands that I am not bound to that woman, I might still have a chance to win her.*

"Bingley, perhaps we can ask Mr. King to assist us. I would like to still teach her a good lesson about stealing, and perhaps we can use this to distance her from us. I plan on giving her the cut direct, as I will not recognize her in public or in private after our discussion. She will never be invited to my homes and if she is at a function where I am, either she must leave or I will. I do not know of Mrs. Hurst's perfidy in this but perhaps it is time," he turned to Mr. Hurst, who was sitting upright and very sober now, "for Hurst to take his rightful place at his family estate and take his wife and sister with him. I believe they have trespassed long enough on your generosity, Bingley." Darcy suggested.

Hurst stood. "Quite right, yes, you are right. I had been too indulgent of my food and drinks and have not taken the reins of my own life. Father has not been feeling well and even though it is a small estate, I do need to take my responsibilities more seriously. Yes, I believe your suggestion is a good one, Darcy. I will remove them after the wedding and return to Liverpool and learn to be a proper landowner."

He was reddened with embarrassment and not inebriation for the first time in years. He bowed and excused himself to make his declarations known to his wife.

Darcy quickly wrote a note to be sent to the King residence and requested his audience.

About an hour later, Mr. King and Richard arrived together, where Darcy informed them of what was discovered and how they would approach Miss Bingley, with Mr. Bingley's full consent.

Darcy wished to run to Lizzy's side but decided to wait until after the situation with Miss Bingley was resolved, so he could give his beloved a full accounting and propose again.

~~*~*~*~*

"How long have you loved her, William?" Georgiana asked, as they sat in his sitting room before facing Caroline Bingley.

Darcy smiled softly. "From the moment I met her. That day of the accident, she came to my rescue, and I hallucinated her looking like Caliban. She was kind and gentle and even though I thought her a hideous monster, I could not help falling in love with her."

His sister asked, "So all those times that you appeared to hate her..."

"Never. I have never hated her. I made a mistake of insulting her several times and even though I tried to explain myself, things became more convoluted until we were both misunderstood. I hope she will accept me. She will be a good sister and it was what you wished for, is it not? To have her as your dear sister?" Darcy beamed.

"Oh, yes, William. It would be my greatest wish. You are the best of brothers and she is the best of sisters." She pulled out their mother's ring, the authentic sapphire, "This will look perfect on Lizzy's hand. Please give this to her as your betrothal ring. It belongs on her finger and never on

Caroline Bingley's."

"But this is your favorite!" Darcy exclaimed.

"Yes, it is, and it will be perfect on my future sister. I will have my replica ring soon enough from that harridan, and perhaps you may trade me *two* other rings for it." Georgiana winked.

Darcy chuckled. "Anything you wish, sweetling. Thank you, it will be perfect for my Lizzy. From one Elizabeth to another."

~~*~*~*~*

"Take a seat, Caroline." Bingley commanded.

Caroline gulped before taking her seat. As nonchalantly as possible, she asked, "What is this about, Charles? Why is Mr. King here? Have you invited him here for dinner without telling me?"

She eyed the angry faces of Mr. Darcy, Miss Darcy, Colonel Fitzwilliam, as well as a sober Mr. Hurst and a very stoic Mr. King. Louisa was cowering in the corner without making eye contact, playing with her bracelet, and Charles loomed over her, as he stood next to her with his hands in tight fists.

Caroline was most afraid of Lady Catherine's presence, whose countenance was unreadable as always. She had heard praises from Miss Darcy and knew that she was Mr. Darcy's favorite aunt, but she had found this grand lady intimidating and frightening whenever they met. She never smiled at her, she never made pleasant conversation, and always scowled at her as if to silently criticize her.

"Well, is this not cozy?" Caroline decided on a preemptive strike. "We must all be gathered for a very special news. All we need is a minister." She nervously laughed. Turning to Mr. Darcy, she spoke confidently with a large, fake smile, "I must assume everyone here knows about our engagement, Mr. Darcy. You must congratulate me, everyone. I am to be Mrs. Darcy."

It was Richard Fitzwilliam who began to laugh first. It was not a laughter of joy but rather a mocking laugh. Caroline's brows furrowed and she fumed at being ridiculed at such an exciting news.

She turned to find her own brother laughing and even Lady Catherine was hiding her amusement.

Caroline began to nervously laugh as well. "Oh, surprise?" She quietly added. Not understanding at all what was happening.

Lady Catherine interrupted the diversion. "I understand I should be congratulating you, Miss Bingley. Not for the betrothal, no, but I hear you are with child. Again. You lost the first one, though? But now you are with child again?" She jibed, "Since we know of no one in this room who will perform such an act with you, who is the father of the baby? Surely not some stable boy or a soldier, I hope."

Caroline turned bright red. "No! Of course, I am not with child! Where did you hear such a ridiculous story?"

Georgiana chimed in next. "From the same source where you spewed your lies, Miss Bingley. Whom you told of your *secret* engagement and that ring you wear as proof of the proposal. Whom you wounded by fabricating a story of a proposal, after an attempt to compromise my brother, then inventing a story of his taking advantage of you. You were with child apparently, but conveniently lost it, only to become with child again, when, William?"

"Last night apparently. You work very quickly. Even if you were sullied last night, it would be impossible to be already with child today. Nothing but lies escaped your mouth, Miss Bingley. Everything you ever said were lies." Darcy spat.

"But we are engaged! Look!" She lifted her hand. "I have your mother's ring. You gave this to me after you begged me to marry you and you took my virtue. You cannot be so dishonorable. Word will spread quickly that you are a rake and where is the honor in that? I know how much your family name means to you. You must marry me!" Miss Bingley shouted in desperation.

Mr. King stood and put his palm out. "Madam, I would like to inspect your ring for authenticity."

Caroline hid her hand away from the man, "But you will not return it to me. This is my only evidence that Mr. Darcy proposed to me. I will not hand it over to you!"

Patiently, the elderly gentleman spoke softly. "I am the magistrate of

Meryton. If this does indeed belong to you because it was gifted to you by its owner, I promise it will be returned to you."

Hesitantly, Caroline pulled the ring from her hand and gave it to the official.

Mr. King inspected it closely, drawing the ring closer to a candlelight, and finished his examination. "Paste. It is a good copy, with its edges carved well to look like a sapphire cut, but it is not real. These are definitely not sapphires and pearls."

Caroline gasped. "Your mother wore paste? Are the shades of Pemberley thus to be polluted? How is it possible that with all her riches, she wore paste?!" She shrieked.

Richard laughed loudly at her again. "You are truly a stupid woman. Why in blazes would my aunt wear paste?" He pointed to Darcy who drew out the original. "Your ring was Georgiana's copy that she purchased in Ramsgate. You stole my cousin's ring, believing that it was Lady Anne's."

Caroline saw the sparkling ring in Darcy's hand and looked over at Mr. King who was still holding the one she had been keeping for the past five months.

"Miss Bingley, you are hereby charged with theft of a personal item valued at one guinea. How do you plead? The penalty, should you be found guilty, is death." Mr. King thundered.

Caroline promptly fainted.

~~*~*~*~*

Caroline awoke to a piercing odor as her sister placed the smelling salts under her nose. She slowly opened her eyes to see that she was lying on the couch in the drawing room.

The room was empty except for Louisa who wore a scowl and as Caroline moaned to sit up, she heard her sister hiss.

"What have you done, Caroline? You are a stupid chit and you could be hanged for your crimes. What were you thinking to steal Miss Darcy's ring? If you had stolen the actual Darcy sapphire, well, you would already be swinging right now. How could you disgrace us like this? And to poison

Mr. Darcy? You could have killed him with your potion. He only fell off his horse because of the draught you put in his coffee. Your maid found the bottle you were hiding in your jewelry box and gave it to Charles. Theft and attempted murder! You are done in society. You will never be able to return to London. I cannot believe I followed your lead all these years only for you to bring us so much shame." Louisa helped Caroline sit up and promptly slapped her cheek.

"OWW! What was that for?" Caroline screeched, as she held her painful cheek.

"You ungrateful chit!" Louisa reddened in anger. She slapped Caroline's other cheek. "I should have been a better elder sister and disciplined you through all your tantrums and whining but I just went along and agreed with you on everything because it was easier. You STOLE from the Darcys, you stupid, stupid girl."

Louisa stood and paced as she continued, "They are at dinner right now and Mr. Hurst is so angry with me for allowing your atrocious behaviors. Everything is in the open now, Caroline. Your attempts to compromise Mr. Darcy, poisoning his coffee, stealing Miss Darcy's ring, all the lies you told Miss Elizabeth about your carrying Mr. Darcy's child," She froze and looked at her sister. "You are not *actually* with child, are you?"

Caroline sat, holding both of her cheeks in pain, with tears running down her face replied, "Of course not! I... I tried to see if I could get with child so I could convince Mr. Darcy that I was carrying his heir but that... that... valet of Mr. Hurst's only laughed at me."

Louisa plopped down most unladylike. "Good Lord! He must be fifty years old!"

"Well, I did not know who else. No one else would agree, even though I tried to get the footman and the stable boy and..." Caroline stopped.

"That is disgusting. Who else?" Louisa spat.

Caroline looked down at her shoes. "Mr... Mr..."

"WHO, Caroline?!" Her sister yelled.

"Mr. Hurst. Your husband." Caroline whispered.

Caroline did not see it coming. She only felt herself swinging backwards as Louisa's fist knocked her out cold.

Chapter 16

"Mr. Bennet, I apologize for calling so early." Darcy shook the elder man's hand.

"It is nothing. Come in, come in. How have you been, Darcy?" He kindly asked.

Darcy took a seat and sighed. "Physically, I am well. I no longer have the headaches and although I still have a block of memory missing, I have enough of a timeline to know what happened now and I am finally free."

Mr. Bennet smiled at the young man. "Yes, it was quite a story you pieced together in your letter last night. I could not have imagined such a thing if I wrote a novel myself." He poured Darcy a cup of tea. "Do you think you will be successful today, son?"

Darcy took a sip of his drink. "I hope so, sir, I truly hope so. Miss Elizabeth and my misunderstandings were so entwined that we continued to cause each other pain, but we have no impediments now. With your blessing, I would like to propose properly and if, no; *when* I am accepted, I would like to marry with Bingley and Miss Bennet in two days. I have sent for a special license already and I am confident that my Uncle Darcy, the judge, will be able to obtain it in time."

Mr. Bennet laughed. "You have my permission, son. I knew you were an upstanding man after spending some time with you going over estate management, and I had guessed that you might be in love with Lizzy then. When you confirmed it when you wrote to me last month, I had no idea you thought she was marrying Collins; just that you could not bear to return here until Bingley's wedding. I would have never guessed my Lizzy loved you in return until Lady Catherine called on us yesterday. Imagine my surprise when that grand lady treated us like family and complimented my wife so graciously on her table design and the furnishings." He pushed some biscuits at Darcy. "It was the first time I heard Lizzy speak kindly of you and her eyes sparkled something I had not seen before."

"I can only hope she loves me as dearly as I love her." Darcy colored shyly. "Lady Catherine is my favorite aunt, sir. My uncle Lord Matlock's wife is well-mannered but takes too much pride in her position. Uncle and Aunt Matlock will not be thrilled that my future wife has no standing in society but they will respect my choice. With Aunt Catherine's approval, they will do their part in promoting Mrs. Darcy and support me. It matters naught; I would marry Lizzy even if every person in the world was against it." Darcy firmly declared. "I truly love her, sir, and she will want for nothing."

Mr. Bennet beamed. "I know, Darcy. I could not have parted with her for anyone less worthy. She is my favorite, you know. Pemberley will be far, but as long as I may visit the grand library when least expected, I heartily approve of your whisking my daughter so far away." He drank his tea. "She should be along shortly. She always peeks in before leaving for her walk and will be quite surprised to see you here."

~~*~*~*~*

Elizabeth froze as soon as she opened her father's door.

Darcy stood with a soft look on his face and the world disappeared as they looked into each other's eyes. Many seconds passed until Mr. Bennet coughed.

Startling into reality, Elizabeth blushed and looked at her father, then back to Darcy. "What are you doing here?"

"I came for you. I received your father's permission for a private audience. May I have a moment of your time?" Darcy gently asked.

She looked at her father, who was smiling and nodding in approval.

With tears rising to her eyes, she nodded.

"You may go to the gardens, Lizzy. Be kind. This young man has been through much yesterday." Mr. Bennet chuckled.

Darcy grinned and proffered his arm and she readily took it.

After donning their coats, Darcy led her patiently to the back corner of the gardens, behind the hedgerows where he had kissed her before, and opened his mouth to speak but Elizabeth's finger was immediately on his lips.

"Yes, my answer is yes. If you will have me, William, I will agree to anything you want from me." Elizabeth smiled as Darcy kissed her finger, and held both of her hands to kiss every one of her fingers. "If you wish for my hand in marriage still, if you can forgive me of all the awful things I said to you, if you still love me..."

Darcy bent to kiss her lips tenderly before she could continue. He leaned his forehead against hers and sighed. "I wish for you more than anything I have ever wanted. I promise to be a good husband to you. I will make you happy. We may argue and disagree often but you will always know I love you. I will be yours and only yours, forever, my love. My dear Lizzy, my beautiful beast."

Elizabeth wrapped her arms around his waist and held him tightly. "As long as you find me *tolerable*, I will always belong to you. I give you my heart and body. Although I do not have much, all I have is yours."

"I need nothing but what I have in my arms, my love. Will you marry me in two days? Will your sister agree to a double wedding?" Darcy eagerly asked.

Elizabeth giggled. "It would give me so much joy to marry you in two days. Jane is the most obliging lady in the world. She will be most happy for us." She lifted her head from his head as they walked back to the middle of the gardens and walked. "Will you tell me what happened yesterday? What did my father mean?"

Darcy kissed her hand while they walked. "I must confess that I have been writing to your father and he knows I have been in love with you a very long time." He smiled at her surprised face. "I told him about how you rescued me and how I insulted you with my hallucinations, but that your kind soul, your inner beauty was irresistible and I could not live without you. Of course in my negligence, I did not ask about your engagement to Collins and I suffered needlessly." He turned to face her. "I would have returned that same day; I would have never left if I knew..." He kissed her hand, "I was a fool to leave. I should have made you listen to me. I should have marched right into Longbourn and called out that fool for daring to stand next to my woman. For even considering to propose to you."

Elizabeth giggled. "I was stubborn-headed and I would have refused to listen. I thought you betrothed to Miss Bingley and could only suffer my own pains alone, even thinking that perhaps once all my sisters were married off, I could offer myself to be your mistress."

"Lizzy, I will never take a mistress, I hope you know that. Although if I had been married already and I met you, I might have been tempted to have you in any way possible, but now that you will be my wife, I will never look to another." Darcy honestly pronounced.

Elizabeth smiled, "Thank you, my love. I know Miss Bingley is very handsome..."

"NO! She is horrid and ugly. She is a terrible human being and you, my love, YOU are the handsomest woman of my acquaintance. I have never touched her, I swear to you. Nothing happened with that woman and I have never thought of doing anything with her. NEVER."

Darcy began to tell her of the events of the evening before and explained how Georgiana's replica ring was stolen.

He laughed as Elizabeth's face was in shock when she heard of Caroline fainting and they both could not hold in their chuckles when he explained how Miss Bingley's nose was broken by her own sister.

"Mr. King was able to threaten her and I had never seen Louisa Hurst so angry before. Apparently, Caroline Bingley tried to seduce Mr. Hurst in his inebriated state to try to breed with him, to pass it off as *my* heir, and Mr. Hurst, not realizing what was happening, fell asleep on top of her, only to suffocate her for a good few minutes before that harpy was able to turn him over and escape to her own rooms. According to that idiotic woman, her virtue remains intact, as no one wanted to go near her, even for a large pay!" Darcy shared what he had heard from Bingley. "Mr. King was grateful to his niece's rescuer and had agreed to teach her a lesson. Wickham will be transferred today and will be out of our lives forever."

Elizabeth took a big breath after calming from her fit of laughter. "I am so glad Wickham did not hurt you, William! He could have seriously wounded you. But it was kind of Mr. King to assist you with Miss Bingley."

"Yes, after Richard helped take care of that blackguard, Mr. King was so grateful that teaching Caroline Bingley a lesson was an easy recompense. She will not be hanged or transported, but will have to forfeit half of her dowry and will be outcasted from society. Richard has already written to his parents to spread word that she is a most awful shrew and that she has offended both Darcys and the future Mrs. Darcy."

Elizabeth smirked. "You were so confident that there would be a 'Mrs. Darcy'? And is Georgiana pleased with such a large reparation?"

"You are the least mercenary woman I have ever met." He kissed her hands. "Georgiana was to receive half and you were to receive the other half," he chuckled as he watched her mouth gape, "but my sister insists that you were the injured party and that you keep everything. Miss Bingley will be banished to her elderly aunt's home in York and will live out the rest of her miserable life in isolation. If she returns to Hertfordshire or enters Derbyshire, or dares to invade any of our homes, she will be transported to the colonies."

"Are you saying that... that I will be given... I thought she told everyone that her dowry was...20..."

Darcy continued for her, "Yes, my love. You will have 10,000 pounds to bring into our marriage."

"Such a sum! I cannot take another woman's dowry! What would I do with such an amount?" She gasped.

Darcy walked her behind the tall bushes and kissed her lips. "You can save it for our children. Our ten daughters will each have 1,000 pound each." He pressed her body tighter to his. "I want to make you my wife desperately, Lizzy, but I swear to you that I have never dallied with anyone. Not a lady, not a servant, not even a prostitute. I saved myself for you and I will know no one else."

Elizabeth melted into his embrace and reveled in his love. "I know, my love. I was a fool. I should have never believed her and should have been truthful with you. I thought you a rake when you began to kiss me but it was my fears of being wanton. I do believe we should marry in two days. I do not wish to wait to be your wife."

Darcy tenderly kissed her lips. "I wish for the same, Lizzy." He knelt down on one knee and presented the beautiful sapphire ring, surrounded by perfectly round pearls, "Since my proposal was so rudely interrupted but thankfully accepted, will you wear this ring to remember my love for you every time you look upon it? Will you be the queen and mistress of my heart for all of time?"

Elizabeth looked down at the ring as he slowly slid the magnificent ring into her finger. It fit perfectly and it shined brighter than anything else she had ever seen.

"It is stunning! It is the most beautiful ring in the world." She proclaimed. "It is similar to Miss Bingl... I mean Georgiana's ring but significantly larger and brighter. I will wear it proudly, William. I could not imagine a better wedding ring."

"Oh, no; this is a betrothal ring. You will have another ring as a wedding band. You will have all the Darcy jewels and can wear a ring in each finger, change them out for every day of the week, and have more left over. My grandfather was an avid collector and it is all yours." Darcy grinned as he stood.

"And you expect me to be dripping with jewels wherever I go? I will look like a dazzling beast with all of my fineries." She teased.

Darcy chuckled. "And I will be the proud man with the most lovely lady on my arm. You are no one's beast but mine." He cradled his hand on Elizabeth's cheek. "You are truly beautiful, inside and out. I love you, my dearest Lizzy."

They returned to the manor where Elizabeth excitedly shared with her father of her acceptance, and as soon as she told Mrs. Bennet of her engagement to a man of 10,000 a year, there was an odd but enjoyable silence in the house, as Mrs. Bennet fainted away from absolute shock.

Chapter 17

"Stop fidgeting, Bingley!" Darcy commanded.

Bingley ceased his movements and replied, "How in the world are you not nervous, Darcy? We will be married men in an hour. ONE HOUR!"

Darcy smiled, "Because I am getting exactly what I wish. I have loved my Lizzy long before you started courting Jane and I cannot wait to be her husband."

"But you never actually courted her. And you and Lizzy were engaged for only two days and will be married today. I do not understand why you are not nervous. This will be life-changing. I will never be the same man ever again after today." Bingley grumbled.

"If you are having second thoughts, tell me now. It will be pistols at dawn for you for jilting my sister-to-be." Darcy sternly commanded.

Bingley nervously laughed. "No, not second thoughts. I just worry..."

"About what, Bingley?" Darcy asked calmly.

Bingley scratched his head. "That we might find something that we do not like about each other, and perhaps discover that we are not compatible. What if we tire of each other and find someone else instead and we are already bound for life? What if she stops loving me because I am a fool? What if I am not enough for her?"

"Charles," Darcy placed his hand on his friend's shoulder, "are you concerned that *you* will tire of her or is it that *she* may not love you later?"

Bingley sat on a chair and rubbed his face vigorously. "My family is a disgrace. I am the son of a tradesman, I am proud of my father, mind you, but I am not a landowner and I have so much to learn still. My sister... my sister Caroline humiliated us and we should all be shamed in public but only thanks to you and Colonel Fitzwilliam, we were able to escape unscathed. Louisa is very regretful and has been a better sister to me but even she is not completely innocent. What if Jane finally realizes what a dishonorable and low family she is marrying into and hates me?"

Darcy smiled and sat in the chair in front of Bingley. "When I was in London, after I fled when Lizzy turned down my first proposal, I had thought for a moment that I might be in love because of the love potion I was given and Lizzy was the first woman to be in my sights. My friend Hastings, asked me these questions and I will ask you the same. Bingley, what is your first thought when you awake? When you fall asleep?"

Bingley smiled softly, staring into space. "I think of Jane. I think of her lovely face and her gentle smile, and I dream of her when I am sleeping. I dream of the adventures we will take and the children we will have. I do love her with all of my heart."

Darcy beamed. "There you have it. If you love her, if you care for her above your own needs, she will have no reason to stop loving you. Whether you argue about something non-consequential, or have to move heaven and earth to be together, if you do not give up on her, she will not give up on you. Take it from me, Bingley, do not lose hope and hold on to what you have. Show your wife every day how you feel about her, through your words and actions, and you will be happy."

Bingley finally smiled. "Thank you, Darcy. Brother. I am very pleased to be gaining a brother and four, no *five*, sisters! I wished for a nice sister like yours and hey, Georgiana will be my sister!" He jovially pronounced.

Darcy laughed, "Yes, the Bennets are most respectable, dowry or not, and they will be a great addition to my small, quiet family. Except for Lady Matlock, who will do as my uncle demands, everyone has been happy for me and I will have no cause to repine. My Lizzy will never want for anything."

Bingley rubbed his fingers on his chin in contemplation, "Say, Darcy, exactly how many times did you propose to Lizzy? I did not know you had proposed at the Ball. I was completely shocked that you became engaged two days ago. I had thought you had not even liked each other but it sounds like you proposed twice? It is unheard of. I cannot believe she refused you the first time."

Darcy chuckled loudly. "I believe I proposed five or six times. I asked her to marry me so many times, I cannot recall exactly how many. I would have asked a thousand times until she agreed if I had known she was not engaged to Collins." He stood. "Now, let us get to church a little early. I may not be nervous but I am most anxious to start my life with my beautiful creature at my side."

~~*~*~*~*

Caroline Bingley had to sit quietly, by her brother's edicts, wearing all of her fineries and looking absolutely resplendent in her orange gown with matching orange feathers, but had to wear a veil to cover her face. Her sister's solid punch had broken her nose and left a massive bruising under both eyes. Louisa and Mr. Hurst absolutely refused to sit with her and oddly enough, everyone in this dull hamlet avoided her. The only one who tolerated sitting next to her was Mr. King and his niece, along with Colonel Fitzwilliam next to that freckled lass who shyly giggled at the uniformed officer when he whispered something that sounded like 'orangutan'.

After the registries were signed, Mr. Hurst practically shoved Caroline Bingley into the awaiting carriage and returned to the wedding party without a word. Miss Bingley could only watch the newlywed Darcys smile at each other, and realization finally dawned upon her that everything she had desired was truly lost, as the carriage rolled away from the merry group.

~~*~*~*~*

"How much longer until we arrive, Mr. Darcy?" Elizabeth asked.

Darcy drew her into his arms and held her tightly. "Another hour to go, Mrs. Darcy. Are you already tired of me, madam?" He teased.

She giggled as she climbed onto his lap and wrapped her arms around his neck. "Not quite yet, sir. Perhaps tomorrow, I will be quite tired of you."

Darcy kissed her lovingly and ran his hands up and down her back. "You will be tired, all right. Hopefully not of me, but definitely tired of my attentions. I guarantee it." He kissed her deeply.

"Well, my courage rises at every attempt to intimidate me. Challenge accepted!" Elizabeth kissed him in return and began to run her fingers through his hair, making him moan loudly until his hand landed on her breast. This time, she moaned into his mouth and they were both huffing for air as they finally separated.

"You make me positively beastly, Lizzy. I lose all semblance of proper behavior when you kiss me like that." Darcy continued to hold her tightly, kissing her neck and running his hand through her hair.

Elizabeth giggled, "You and I will be beastly together, William. I will be your loathsome beast and you will be my handsome beast."

"Oh, no, you are definitely *la Belle* and I am *la Bête*. We have known that for a very long time." Darcy responded.

Elizabeth jumped at this. "I loved that book! Have you read it in French?"

Darcy grinned broadly, "Yes, I had begun it after my accident but Richard told me to read more poetry. I did finish the English translation."

They spoke merrily of the book and discussed it for the next hour and soon enough, they arrived at Darcy House.

~~*~*~*~*

"Georgiana had told me about Darcy House but I could not have imagined this! It is a beautiful home!" Elizabeth gushed.

Darcy held her from behind, kissing her temple as he wrapped his arms around her torso. "And of all this you are now mistress. And you will have

Pemberley and Kieran Hall and Manchester Lodge to care for as well. But you will not have to worry about any of the estates at all. You have only one task required of you and I care not if you sit on your silk cushions and eat chocolate all day, as long as you fulfill your *one* duty."

"And what may that duty be, Mr. Darcy?" Elizabeth turned around to wrap her arms around her husband's neck.

He leaned down and kissed her tenderly. "Why, to make Mr. Darcy happy, of course. And you are doing it right now. You, here in my arms, I have never known such happiness."

Darcy led his wife to the mistress' chamber where they did not wait to partake a meal or to wait for darkness to fall; they loved each other and joined as man and wife in body as soon as the doors closed.

~~*~*~*~*

"It was so kind of Aunt Catherine to host Georgiana for a fortnight, but I cannot wait to see her again." Elizabeth exclaimed.

"She has been very happy for us, my love, but I know she is eager to see us as well. Anne has enjoyed the company and is excited to finally meet you this afternoon. You will see your friend, the former Miss Lucas, at Hunsford and you will love Rosings. It is second only to Pemberley, in my humble opinion."

Elizabeth began to laugh, "Since when have you had a single humble opinion? You just praised your own home!"

Darcy tickled her, "Our home, my love. I am only humble when it comes to you. Otherwise I am still a proud, haughty man, who will only bend to my wife's will and no one else's."

Elizabeth kissed his cheeks. "As long as you are with me, we will be proud together. I am so happy, William."

"I know I have been quite beastly, Lizzy. You are well? Are you tired of me yet?" Darcy kissed her neck as they lay together in bed and he caressed her naked body again.

"Never. I enjoy your attentions more than I ever thought possible. I love joining with you and learning new ways to make love. Mama told me to lie back and stay still but how wrong she was. You feel so good, my love." Elizabeth could not continue, as her husband began to love her again.

"I love you, Mrs. Darcy." Darcy softly whispered.

"I love you, Mr. Darcy." Elizabeth replied in his ear.

Epilogue

Elizabeth and Darcy spent the next month at Rosings, where Elizabeth and Anne de Bourgh's friendship grew and they would write to each other whenever apart for the next four years until Anne's demise.

Lady Catherine would often travel to Pemberley and the Darcy children called her 'grandmama' in lieu of 'great aunt' due to their closeness. When she passed twenty years later, she was celebrated as a generous and kind lady and she left Rosings to Darcy's second son. Mr. Collins cried copiously while he conducted the funeral but Charlotte Collins stood by his side and consoled him and cried with him, missing the great lady's guidance during all of the years she had helped her mold her husband into a better man.

Mr. and Mrs. Bingley were happily situated in Netherfield where they resided for twelve months after their wedding, and they were most delighted when a property only twenty miles from Pemberley became available for purchase. Elizabeth was thrilled to have her dearest sister nearer, and Jane was elated to be mistress of Winterfall Estate without the constant disruptions of her mother.

Jane bore twin sons, Charles Jr. and Caleb Bingley, and a daughter, Lizbeth Bingley, and they lived blissfully together, making frequent visits to Pemberley and being so complying, never exceeding their income but always so generous that no servant ever cheated them.

Richard Fitzwilliam courted and married Mary King three months after Darcy's wedding, and his mother was so pleased with her favorite son's wife that she promoted the new Mrs. Richard Fitzwilliam, as she had done with Elizabeth Darcy, and society could do naught but follow the countess' example. Taking these two women as examples, it became fashionable to take walks for pleasure and to become slightly brown during the summer months. Freckles were now considered chic, and some even went to the trouble of drawing their own onto their faces.

Caroline Bingley spent the next five and thirty years in York and took over the house when her Aunt Bingley passed away. She became the leader of the small society there with all of her accomplishments, but failed to capture any suitors and she remained unmarried for the rest of her life. She was only grateful that she was able to live a long and healthy life, instead of being hanged in the gallows as a criminal, which was kept a secret from all her friends. She never returned to London but could only envy reading about news of her family and those she recognized from the gossip columns.

Mary Bennet was surprisingly courted by Lieutenant Denny who, being the second son of a parson, appreciated the calm demeanor of this quiet middle child, and Mary entertained her fellow officers' wives with singing and dancing in the various encampments to which they traveled.

Georgiana married two years after her coming out, not settling for those who might court her favors for her dowry and connections. She had unfortunately slipped and sprained her ankle and Darcy called for his friend to treat his dearest sister.

Doctor Hastings urgently looked at Georgiana's ankle and finding it a sprain, sighed in relief and looked up to find his friend's little sister transformed into a beautiful young lady. He immediately gulped and excused himself from Mrs. Darcy, who had been keeping Georgiana company, and ran to Darcy, pacing like a mad man.

When Darcy was able to finally sort out what was bothering his friend, he laughed out loudly, informing Hastings that his baby sister was no longer a child and with proper intent, would allow a courtship if Georgiana agreed.

Georgiana had been in love with the doctor ever since their residing at Netherfield together after Darcy's accident, and although she had thought it a passing fancy, she could not find anyone more worthy, even after her official coming out two years ago.

Georgiana married the good doctor four months later and using her dowry, they established hospitals to help the destitute and became one of the most charitable couples in England.

Kitty and Lydia grew to be calm, demure ladies, unrecognizable from the wild and unruly children that they once were. They were most happy to be courted by brothers and married in a double ceremony, with Mrs. Bennet nearly fainting at the excitement of having two daughters marry brothers at the same time. Mrs. Bennet praised Miss Darcy for throwing her daughters in the paths of rich men and always treated Georgiana like another daughter, caring for her and filling that void of the orphan, by being like a parent to the elegant young lady whenever they visited each other.

Mr. Bennet was also like a father to both Darcy and Georgiana, always lending a patient ear and becoming a great correspondent through letters with his favorite son-in-law. With Darcy's advisement, Mr. Bennet took Mr. Collins by his side to educate him on how to manage Longbourn, and after Lady Catherine's passing, he allowed Mr. and Mrs. Collins to take over the estate so he could have more time to travel with Mrs. Bennet.

Mr. and Mrs. Bennet lived in harmony for another decade when Mrs. Bennet predeceased him, thankfully never being tossed into the hedgerows, and Mr. Bennet lived out the rest of his life in the comforts of the Pemberley library, surrounded by his favorite daughter, son-in-law, and his grandchildren.

Darcy and Elizabeth had three daughters, followed by two sons. Elizabeth feared that she might be like her mother in giving her husband only daughters, but Darcy emphasized again and again that he wished for ten daughters and it mattered naught if they had no sons. Elizabeth was extremely relieved to bear their heir, Bennet Darcy, and cried with joy when Daniel Darcy was born.

Darcy and Elizabeth still argued and misunderstood each other often but never let the sun go down while still angry. They spoke openly of their worries and fears so they would accept each other's faults and mistakes, while still loving each other with all of their hearts and committing to the other's happiness before themselves.

~~*~*~*~*

"How would you feel if I was still that horrid monster you first met and it was only a hallucination these past twenty years of seeing me more handsome, William?" Elizabeth asked her husband, as they sat to watch the sunrise as they had done every morning.

Darcy chuckled. "You ask the strangest questions, Lizzy." He gathered her into his embrace. "No matter how you appear, my little beast, I have loved you from that first day and I would not change a thing. Even when you looked deformed and freckled, I thought you lovely and wanted to kiss you." He leaned and kissed her lips tenderly. "Even after twenty years of being married to the most loathsome creature I have ever seen, OWW!" Darcy rubbed his arm where she pinched him, "you bring me more joy than anything I could have ever imagined."

Elizabeth giggled, "I wonder if I had hallucinated you as a monster, if I would have loved you. You were quite arrogant, ordering me about like a servant and demanding me to bend to your will."

"Well, here we are, the Proud and the Beast, happily married and expecting our first grandchild. Let us return and see if our duchess daughter will give us a grandson or a granddaughter." He helped her stand and walked with her hand on his arm. "No matter boy or girl, that child will be cherished, just like I cherish all our children."

"I love you, Mr. Darcy." Elizabeth leaned her head on his arm. "You are the best of men."

Darcy smiled, "I love you, Mrs. Darcy. You are the best of beasts. OWW!" He yelped, as she pinched his arm again.

Printed in Great Britain
by Amazon

45351835R00057